I0769448

THE OLD MILL PAINTINGS

THE OLD MILL PAINTINGS

Larry Engels

Deeds Publishing | Athens

Published by Deeds Publishing in Athens, GA
www.deedspublishing.com

Printed in The United States of America

Cover and interior design by Deeds Publishing

ISBN 978-1-961505-10-0

Books are available in quantity for promotional or premium use. For information, email info@deedspublishing.com.

First Edition, 2023

10 9 8 7 6 5 4 3 2 1

To my dear departed wife Cynthia

*She gave me The Old Mill Painting
and was inspiration in all my writing's.*

Contents

1. The Assignment

David thought to himself: *I sure hope I don't fall asleep in this class. If this were one of the large auditorium classes, I could just sleep away on the back row. Alas, with only about forty students, my professor would notice me sleeping for sure. I must get more sleep at night.* It was hard, but he managed to at least appear to stay awake.

"Alright students, I am passing out the information on your final term paper for your English 101 class. As many of you may know, starting last year I made this a requirement for the final 20% of your grade in this course. What I want is a minimum three-thousand-word paper on any subject you choose. The subject you choose must require research by you, using any media you wish. You will be required to list research sources you used. Don't even think of trying to use a paper from previous classes, as I have a pretty fair memory," Professor Murphy stated.

"You are to submit your proposed subject for my approval by next Tuesday, April 20th and the essay will be due on May 5th. You may bounce research ideas off each other but the writing is to be your own. The purpose of this assignment is to help you gain a better understanding of the importance of research and correct use of the English language in business writing."

Well at least his tough old professor had given him a writing assignment, though lengthy, one that appeared easier. That last one, to correctly use every punctuation in only one hundred and fifty words was tough, David remembered.

"That's all for today, class. I will see you on Monday." The professor ended with, "Have a good weekend."

Sure right, give us a major project then wish us a nice weekend. Not cool, David thought as he prepared to depart Professor Murphy's classroom.

"So, David what are you going to choose for a topic," Sandy asked him as he was packing up his book bag.

"Have not the foggiest idea, this is going to be such a pain in the butt. I have summer to get excited about and didn't need this to take away from that, not to mention having to do this whole studding for other exams," he added.

Sandy came back with, "Well you know it could be interesting if you picked the right subject. I would be willing to help you choose one if you like."

"Thanks for the offer, Sandy. I will see if I come up with anything this weekend. See you on Monday."

David thought: *Sandy is sure pushy. I should just blow her off, but since I am somewhat between girlfriends now, I had better try and be nice to her for a spell. She is rather cute, perhaps I should ask her out.*

"Say, David, you going to join us up at the lake this weekend?" John asked, as they made their way to the parking lot.

"No, wish I could. I am supposed to help my dad move some stuff to one of those storage places on Saturday. You guys' camping out, or staying at the house?"

"We have the house," John said.

"Will you still be there on Sunday? If so, I could probably run up there for the afternoon," David added.

"Sorry man, Bill has to be back for some doings that afternoon so we will be leaving in the morning. Maybe next time," John responded.

David enjoyed going up to John's parents' vacation house at the lake with friends. There had been some pretty wild parties at the lake. David especially liked taking John's sailboat out, that is, when the wind was just right. After getting becalmed once while out on the lake with a girl and having to paddle the boat back, he now knew to verify the wind forecast before sailing.

Saturday morning, David and his dad were loading up his dad's large SUV with a bunch of heavy boxes of books and other junk to take to a nearby storage warehouse. He decided to ask his dad for an idea of a subject he might use for his English paper. His dad had written a book or two so David felt he might have some good ideas.

"Dad, I have to write this essay for my English class. The professor told us to pick a subject that would require some research. You got any good idea what might be a good topic?"

"Your professor didn't give you any examples of what he was looking for?" his dad inquired.

"No, that was pretty much it, sort of open ended."

His father said he would think about it. A short time

later, while driving to the warehouse he responded, "David, as you know I have really gotten into our family genealogy recently. I have been trying to get you interested in your ancestry as well. Would you consider researching a distant relative and writing about them?"

"You know, that might just be a good idea. Probably no one else would think of something like that. Do you have any likely suspects from our family tree," David inquired.

"Well, son when we get through here and get back home, I will show you the work I have done on our ancestry and perhaps we can find a relative for you to research. I am sure we have some eccentric ones amongst the skeletons in our family closet," he added.

"No dad, I don't want to write about some family murderer or such," David joked.

"Hopefully we don't have any murderers, but I am sure we have some eccentrics," his dad added.

That night David's father, Brad, pulled out his family research. His mother, Alice, joined in the discussion of their heirs. Alice's family tree was pretty complete back to the seventeenth century in Scotland and Ireland. There seemed to be more unknowns on his father's 'Mack' family line.

"David, here is a possibility for you. Your grandfather had a brother, Henry Mack. He would have been your great uncle. I am sure he is probably dead now since his brother, your grandfather, is. My father said his brother Henry was rather strange and eccentric. I tried to ask my father more about him before he died. Apparently, he and Henry were not close and he didn't want to talk about him much.

I thought about trying to research Henry but never did. About the only things I remember my father saying was something about an old mill he may have once owned and that maybe he was a painter of sorts," David's father added.

"Dad, Henry sounds like he might be an interesting individual to research and write about. Perhaps I can find out something about him on that Ancestry.com website," David said. "Dad you wouldn't mind springing for an 'Ancestry' subscription, would you?"

"For you son, why not. Guess we can just consider it part of your school expense; besides I am curious what you might turn up about our relative," he added.

The following Tuesday, David submitted his great uncle, Henry Mack, as his subject to research for his paper.

What followed was two weeks of nightly research. Unfortunately, he didn't discover as much about his relative as he would have liked. He, therefore, took a little literary license in writing about him. He carefully crafted his writing, trying not to have any of the grammatical or spelling mistakes that he was so well known for in his English classes. David really needed a good grade on the paper. He was hoping to get his present 'C' average up to a 'B'. David felt confident when he submitted it to Professor Murphy on the due date.

David was expecting to have his end of semester grade for his English 101 class posted by May 15th. Instead, he received an unexpected e-mail from professor Murphy requesting he meet him at his office at 9 am on Friday, May 10th. David cringed. Why on earth did the professor want to meet with him. Had his paper been that bad? Had he failed the class? David was very unnerved as he waited for that appointment.

He arrived at the professor's office about fifteen minutes early. The professor's secretary said Professor Murphy had not arrived yet and she told him to take a seat and that the professor should be in shortly. Soon after he was seated, a very attractive girl arrived. As David was staring at this lovely blond, he heard her tell the secretary that she was there for a 9 am appointment with professor Murphy. The secretary likewise told her to also be seated.

By then, curiosity joined the stress David was experiencing. Finally, David said, "Hi, I am David Mack, guess we are both here to see Professor Murphy, only I don't know why, do you know why we are here?"

"Not a clue," the pert young woman answered. "Nice to meet you David. My name is Jill Howard. Say, did you say your last name is Mack?" she asked.

Before they could continue any further exchange, Professor Murphy walked in. His secretary told him two students were there to meet him. Without her giving the professor their names, he said, "Hello, Jill and David, hope you haven't been waiting long. Come on into my office and be seated."

The professor opened the conversation by saying, "My guess is that you, Jill, know David here, am I correct?"

"No sir, we just met," Jill responded.

"That's right," David added.

"Well, well, that does make this whole thing even more curious," the professor stated.

"I know you are both in different classes of mine, but

you didn't exchange ideas on what to write about?" he again asked.

"No sir," they both responded.

"You see I have had some students use other students work before. Of course, that is a big no, no. I tell classes they can bounce ideas off each other, but the work must be theirs. I can't ever recall when two students appear to have, by chance, written about the same unique subject as you two seem to have. To think, you were in separate classes as well. At this point, if the two of you don't mind, I would like to give each of you a copy of the other's essay. Is that, OK?"

"Yes, Sir, that will be fine," they both responded.

Professor Murphy then added, "I believe you two may find you have something in common."

"Oh, and by the way, you both wrote excellent papers and I gave each of you an 'A'. David, I must add, you probably should learn to spell your professor's names correctly," Professor Murphy added.

David, blushed, saying, "Sorry, sir."

With that, he gave copies of each other's papers to them. The three of them then visited and David and Jill thanked him for their grades. As David walked Jill to her car he said, "Wow, what are the odds we accidently wrote about pretty near the same subject? Amazing!"

"David, when we were waiting for the professor and you said your last name was Mack, I knew something strange was about to happen," Jill commented.

"Well, you were right about that!"

David asked Jill if she might like to get together and

talk after they had read each other's papers. She seemed surprisingly excited to do so. They exchanged cell phone numbers as they departed.

2. The Essays

David could hardly wait to get home after his last class that afternoon so he could read Jill's essay. What on earth could she have written that was connected with his relative? He wondered. Her essay started with her describing a beautiful old oil painting of an old grist mill. Immediately it hit him. The painting she wrote about was signed with the name of H. Mack. David was shocked. Could that be Henry Mack?

He read on as she described what she had discovered about how her family had come into possession of the painting. Apparently, the artist had given it to a great aunt of hers some twenty-five or so years earlier. Her aunt was now dead but had left it to her father with some other items. As for the artist, she said her research showed that he painted in Tennessee and North Carolina as well as other scenic areas. It seemed that he was apparently somewhat of a recluse. She had found records of a few other works by him but no other mention of old mill paintings. She had not found what the connection was between her great aunt and the artist H. Mack.

In closing, she had discovered the artist had passed

away apparently in 1995 at an age of fifty- nine though no obituary or surviving family were mentioned. David thought it curious Jill did not list Ancestry.com in her research sources. He thought, if she had, she would likely have found out more about him as he had.

How strange, Jill had one of his great uncle's paintings. He must ask her to let him see it when they next got together. To think this beautiful girl admired a painting that a relative of his had painted. *What a great source of an introduction, he thought.*

Jill also was anxious to read David's paper and had thoroughly devoured it by that evening. She was totally shocked to find that David had written about the artist of her painting. Even more so that the artist had been David's relative. How utterly amazing that they had both chosen the subjects they had, she thought. Jill pondered this being some sort of a sign. She anxiously awaited a call from David and decided if he hadn't called her by the next day, she would call him.

Jill, not having a boyfriend in town at present, left her wondering about David. He was handsome and did seem like a nice guy. She wondered if he was seriously involved with a girl.

David had finished reading Jill's essay, and it was eight-thirty. He thought about whether it might be too late to call her that night. Just as quickly he decided it wasn't. He was glad that he had enough wits about him that morning to get her phone number. Somewhat nervously, he entered her number in his cell and gave her a call.

To his surprise, she answered right away. "Hey Jill, are you as shocked as I am?"

"Yah, just unbelievable. So, my painting's artist was your great uncle. How very, very strange. What are the odds?" she said.

"Pretty darn long. To think of all the subjects you could have chosen to write about, and you chose that particular painting. And all the people or things I could have chosen and I chose a weird great uncle," David responded.

"Why do you call him weird? He was a very talented painter," Jill commented.

"You really think so? I would sure like to see your painting,"

"Well, I will show it to you when you pick me up for dinner. That is what you were calling me about, wasn't it?" she laughed.

"Just a little forward, aren't you, my girl? How do you know I don't have a girlfriend who might object, not to mention some boyfriend of yours who might want to pound on me?"

"Well, you are probably too weird to have a girlfriend, and me, perhaps I am too tired of fighting off men at present," she quipped.

"You are sure full of yourself and such a mind reader. Just where am I planning to take you to dine, and oh yes, when will we be doing this dining thing? If I might ask?" he joked.

"How about tomorrow night? I could pick you up at six-thirty if that is ok."

"Yes, six thirty tomorrow night will be fine," Jill responded.

"Seriously do you have a favorite type of food or place you like?" David asked.

"Oh, I like a lot of different foods. How about Italian, and six-thirty will be great."

"Italian, it is. I happen to know of a really good Italian spot. Have you been to Casa Rustica, by chance?" David asked.

"No but if you like it, I am sure it will be fine".

"Say, Jill, before we go, I guess you probably should tell me where you live. Do you live with your parents?"

"Sure, it does make sense to give you my address. Presently I am living at home but plan to get an apartment with a girlfriend in the fall. See you tomorrow at six-thirty."

As David hung up the phone, he was pretty proud of himself. In one day's time he had met a beautiful girl with whom he had something in common, and he even had a date with her. Besides that, he had just gotten an 'A' on his paper. Boy, was he excited.

David had yet to tell his parents about the remarkable coincidence of the girl writing an essay about the painting his father's uncle had painted. Since he was too excited to sleep and since his dad was still up, he decided to tell him about Jill and her painting.

"Dad, you know you suggested I research and write about your Uncle Henry. Well guess what, so did another student, in a manner of speaking. There is this girl in another English class with my professor who wrote about a painting that Uncle Henry seems to have painted. The professor connected us. I have a date with her tomorrow night. She is very attractive and seems quite nice."

"David, did you say she has one of Uncle Henry's paintings?" his father asked.

"Yes, it is a painting of an old grist mill, I think. She is going to show it to me tomorrow when I pick her up for our date."

"Well, David, that is sure one amazing coincidence. That painting must be by Uncle Henry because he apparently had a thing for old grist mills. I think somewhere we have another of his paintings of an old grist mill. Let me ask your mother if she knows where it might be," his father said as he left their den. Shortly his mother and father both returned.

"David, your father said you wanted to see that old mill painting that used to hang in the den in our old house. I never cared for it too much. I felt it was a bit dark, though it may have just needed a good cleaning. I believe it is stored in the storage room in the basement, if you wish to see it. Since it is late tonight, you may want to wait and go looking in the morning," his mother suggested.

"Well, yes, it is late, but I believe I am going to look for it now. This whole story is just so odd. I will rest better once I see the painting," David commented.

With that, David began his search for the painting. About an hour later, he found the painting. His parents having gone to bed, he took the painting upstairs to his bedroom. His mother was right, it did appear a bit dark.

Probably a good cleaning would make it look a lot better, but still it was quite beautiful.

The painting was oil on a board and enclosed in an old sculptured frame. It was a quite captivating old grist mill, with a boy fishing in a stream beside the mill. Of particular note in the painting was the stream tumbling vigorously over boulders, creating ripples and waves which shone in the sunlight.

On examining the painting further, he noted some very curious writing on the back side of the painting. The note read 'and it's yours.' He pondered what possibly that note could mean?

Finally, all the day's exciting happenings took their toll and David finally got to sleep early in the morning. Fortunately, he had only one final exam the next day. It was a beginning Engineering Lab and he had a solid 'B' average in that class. With the afternoon free, he could daydream about his date, then shower. He realized he might need to make a dinner reservation. That would be a sign to her that he planned ahead and was a sophisticated guy.

As David drove through the lavish entry gate of Jill's subdivision, he anticipated that her parents probably had a really grand home. Upon finding the address his suspicion was confirmed. The house was a sprawling two, perhaps, three story home with a stone and wood exterior. He carefully pulled into the driveway in front of their three-car garage.

David had thought that since he had already met Jill at the professor's office, this wouldn't actually be a blind date.

Still, he was a bit uncertain about the date and somewhat nervous.

When he rang the doorbell, Jill was there to answer the door. David said, "Wow, you look beautiful."

"Thanks, you look great yourself." *He then wondered if he should have brought her flowers. Then realized probably not for a first date.*

"Come on in, David, and meet my folks," she said as she showed him in to their Great Room.

"Hello, David, I am Jason Howard," her father said, while giving him the firm handshake of a protective father. "This is my wife, Mary. Jill tells us your relative painted the old mill oil painting over there," he said, while pointing to the painting hanging on the far wall.

"That's what I understand, sir," David responded as he made his way toward the painting.

"I still can't quite believe the coincidence," Jill commented

"Truly amazing," her mother interjected as all four were gazing upon the old painting.

"Mr. and Mrs. Howard, and Jill, I have another surprise. Unbeknownst to me, my father also has another oil painting by Henry Mack of what appears to be the very same old mill. If you don't mind, I will get it out of my car, so we can compare them," David said.

"That will be great, but David please call us by our first names, Jason and Mary."

Jill, quite excitedly said, "Yes, David, please do bring it in. We would love to see it."

They all commented how it was obviously the same

mill and painted by the same artist. They also took note that David's was slightly smaller than the one Jill's family owned. After everyone commented on the two paintings. David said, "I discovered a strange note on the back of my family's painting." He turned the painting over, revealing a penned note in the lower corner which read, 'and it's yours'. "Do you have any idea what the note might mean?"

Jill piped up, "I wonder if ours has a strange note on it? Let me take it down and check."

With her father's help, she carefully lifted the three-foot-wide painting. Turning it over, sure enough there was a mysterious handwritten note in the same lower right corner. It read, 'Find my mate'.

David was the first to say, "If you put that note together with the note on mine, it would read 'Find my mate—and it will be yours'. This has to be some clue to something, don't you think, but what?"

Now everyone was quite curious at the strange inscriptions. Each started offering thoughts as to what these might mean.

Jill commented, "From my research on Henry Mack, he was an eccentric individual who avoided publicity, so there was not much telling."

David spoke up, "That was the same impression I formed from my research. It is something exciting to ponder. Where did you come by your painting?" David asked.

"Oh, I believe it may have come from the estate of an old relative of my wife. Mary, do you remember the name of who left it to us?" Jason asked.

"That was so long ago. The name Carolyn seems to ring a bell," she commented.

David noticed the time. "Jill, our dinner reservation is in fifteen minutes, so perhaps we should go."

"Jason and Mary, it has been great to meet you," David commented.

Her parents bid them well, saying, "You two will have something mysterious to discuss over dinner. Have fun. Great to meet you, David."

David, acting the gentleman, opened the car door for Jill. As they drove, he somewhat nervously started the conversation, "Jill, have you never been to this restaurant Casa Rustica?"

"No, but I do especially like Italian food. Even though it can be a bit fattening," she added.

"Well, with your figure you look in great shape so I don't expect a little tasty pasta will turn you into a blimp. Besides, with that beautiful blond hair and that captivating smile of yours, you would be beautiful if you were a blimp." She laughed at that. A good sign he thought.

Jill, being the slightly more outgoing of the pair, led into a conversation by saying, "So David, you know this is sort of like a blind date. We don't know much about each other. What are you studying in college?"

"I am presently in Civil Engineering," he responded.

"Oh, so you are a Dam man," she joked.

They both laughed.

"I guess you could say that. That description is better than 'potty piper' as one of my friends call me," David commented.

"Really, he calls you that?" she laughed.

"Yah that is Bill's nickname for me. I don't much care for it though."

"I can certainly understand that," she said.

What about you, Jill, what are you studying?"

"Well, that is an interesting and I guess embarrassing question. The answer is, I haven't actually decided. I am torn between Education, Creative Writing, Business Management, and even Veterinary Medicine. So, this year I am trying to take courses that I would need for any degree. I must declare a major by next fall though. Any thoughts?" Jill asked.

"That is not an answer I would have guessed. Such a wide variety. All quite interesting, I would say. That answer gives me an answer to another question though. It seems, like me, you must like animals," David commented.

"Yes, I do like animals, large and small. I have a dog and cat at home," she said.

David continued, "To be honest, although I am presently in Civil Engineering, I have considered changing to Architecture or even Building Construction. My career choice has been a tough decision. I think too many young adults tend to follow their parents' careers or pursue what their parents suggest, rather than follow their own dreams, don't you think?"

Before Jill could respond, they arrived at the restaurant and had to postpone the career conversation until they were seated and had ordered.

"Jill, I do hope you like the food here. I have been here a couple of times and I found it great. What are some of your favorite places to eat?"

"Hard question, as I said, I like a variety of foods. For Chinese, I like The House of Ing," she announced before the waiter interrupted their conversation.

"Well, I guess we better think Italian presently," David commented as they looked over the menus discussing various entrees. Soon they had settled on both going with the spicy Chicken Cacciatore.

"You know, I will sure be glad when we are legal so we could have a glass of wine with dinner. Have you ever had any wine, Jill?" he asked.

"For sure, yes, I have tasted wine before. I think I prefer white wine. What about you, red or white?" she asked.

"Agreed, I prefer white but rosé is nice. Don't care too much for red. The red I had was a bit strong tasting. I feel the same about beer. I don't like strong tasting beer."

"David, what about family, do you have any brothers and sisters?" Jill asked.

"Nope, it's just me. How about you, any siblings?" he asked.

"Well, I do have one sister, Janet, who is a bit older. She and I get along pretty well but she is always playing tricks on me. She is attending college out of state and will be home soon for the summer. Perhaps you can meet her," Jill added.

"Sure, I would love to meet her."

"Jill, what are your summer plans?" David asked.

"My mother has a florist shop and she wants me to help her with it this summer. I like flowers and so it should be a pretty enjoyable job. She is going to pay me the same wage as her other employees. I know what you are thinking, what does working in a florist shop have to do with my career interests. Well, nothing," she admitted, "but still, it will be fun working with my mom. David, what about you? What are your summer plans?"

"One of my CE professors has a sideline surveying business. I enjoyed the surveying class I took my last semester so it will be good experience, I believe. Since I aced his class, he offered me a job for the summer on a survey crew. Guess I will spend the summer in the woods with the snakes and insects. Hopefully, it won't be too bad. I do like the outdoors, you know, camping and such," David explained. "Speaking of outdoors do you by chance like hiking and camping, Jill?" he asked.

"I do, I have not had a lot of opportunity but when I was younger, I did hike some with my family. We probably would have done more but my sister hated it. So, we did other things instead. It is really amazing in how many ways we are so different," she joked. "Janet is more impetuous, self-centered, and prone to making irrational decisions. She jumps from one thing to the next without ever focusing long on anything. She is studying music at college. Time will tell if she sticks with that," Jill concluded.

As they were finishing their meals, their conversation returned to the paintings and how they met. David said, "I would like to try and find out just what the message on the back of the paintings means. Are you interested in helping solve the mystery?"

"You bet. It will be an exciting adventure to try and figure it out. Looks like we both hold clues to the mystery.

Should be a lot of fun getting to the bottom of it. So, what do we do next?" she asked.

"I am so glad you agree we need to solve the mystery of the paintings. I believe with the work we have both put in, we should be well on our way to figuring the whole thing out. Apparently, my great uncle had just such an adventure in mind with those two paintings. I believe we will make a good pair of detectives. I can see us having a lot of fun along the way," David said while smiling at Jill.

Jill laughed saying, "You think?"

When David drove her home that evening, he struggled with whether to kiss her goodnight. It was only their first date and all. She was just so sweet and irresistible. He decided to just go for it. He really wanted to, so he did. Surprisingly, she was very receptive. He left her house on cloud nine. He appeared to have a great adventure ahead and more importantly, perhaps a really swell new girlfriend.

3. Double Trouble – The Sister

The semester had ended and finally school was over until fall. Summer had arrived. Was David ever glad. The last week or so was tough what with exams and all. Now he had the summer to look forward to, even if it meant he had a fulltime summer job that would take up a great bit of his fun time. But then, there was Jill and the mystery for the pair to solve. Wow! Was it ever going to be fun working on the mystery with her.

It had been over a week since his first date with Jill. Though David had spoken with her by phone a couple of times they had not been able to get together again due to exams. Jill had already started her job helping her mother in the flower shop.

Jill called David on a Thursday evening. "Say, David do you have plans for Saturday night?"

"No, what are you thinking?" David asked.

"Well, I thought I might fix us some dinner. Afterwards, if you want to, we might discuss ideas about starting our research on the Old Mill. It turns out my parents are taking another couple up to our mountain cabin for the weekend so they will be gone on Saturday. My sister is back in town but I am sure she will be out with friends. She always is. So, we will have the house to ourselves. I plan to close the shop at 5:00, go to the grocery, then freshen up, so why don't you plan to come over about 6:30. We can make dinner together, if you like," Jill said.

"Sounds like a great plan, though I am afraid I am not much of a cook. Hope you are," David said. "What can I bring?"

"Just yourself. I plan to smuggle out a bottle of my parents' wine for us as well," she responded.

"Wow, that will be a treat … a home cooked dinner and illicit wine to boot."

David was overjoyed with the thought of such an intimate time with her. Though he did not know Jill very well yet, he was already smitten with her.

Saturday morning, David received another call from Jill's parent's number. He thought it strange she was calling on a house phone instead of her cell. Perhaps her phone was charging, he thought.

"Hi David, Jill here, I will be closing the shop an hour earlier than I had planned so why don't you come over an hour earlier, say at 5:30."

David responded that he could do that and he would see her then. He rushed about getting ready. He thought about taking her some flowers, but he decided against that, seeing as how she had been dealing with flowers all day at work. He was really looking forward to seeing her again.

Jill answered the door, giving him a big hug and welcoming him in.

"You have had your hair done. Your hair is different. I

like it. Glad you are not one of those gals who puts crazy colors in your hair."

"Yeh, did that once. Parents flipped out," she said.

"Thanks, glad you like my hair. Wanted it shorter for summer. Long hair hanging down on my neck in summer is a pain," she responded.

"But you have such beautiful blond hair," he commented.

"I missed you," she said, right before further surprising him by throwing her arms around him and giving him another big hug. Even more surprising, she gave him a big wet kiss.

"Well, it's good to see you missed me. I must remember to stay away more often," he mused.

She told him to take a seat on a sofa in their great room. She then rushed off to the kitchen. Quickly she returned with two wine glasses and a bottle of red wine.

"Oh, I see it's red wine tonight. I though you preferred white wine," he commented.

"Oh well, I just drink what is available," she shockingly responded.

David wondered at how open she was about her underage drinking. After a few swallows of wine, she casually asked, "How about a little sex before dinner? Or would you prefer your dessert later?"

David was completely shocked by her offer of sex. After a moment's hesitation he responded, "How much wine have you had before I got here? This is quite unlike what I would have expected of you. I don't know what to say. Why don't we just enjoy our wine and dinner then we can think about sex."

In an attempt to change the subject, David asked, "What are we eating for supper. Since you served red wine, are we having red meat perhaps?"

Unfortunately, his attempt at a subject change failed.

"Forget food, me be horny now!" She said, while moving closer to him on the couch. She then started French kissing him. David tried to politely put a bit more distance between the pair.

By this time, David was becoming quite alarmed at her forwardness. Perhaps he had really not known her at all, he thought. Her aggressive behavior, rather than turning him on was having the opposite effect. While all this display of affection was going on, neither of them were aware that someone had entered the kitchen from the garage. Suddenly, the real Jill appeared in the doorway.

"What the hell! Janet, what are you doing with my boyfriend, David?" She admonished her twin in a very angry voice.

"Oh, hi sis," David's kissing mate said.

David, having by then jumped up, responded, "Jill, who the hell is this? I thought she was you."

"Oh! You mean my, soon to be deceased twin sister there! Has she molested you too badly. If so, we shall take turns pounding on her," she said.

David then, in a completely embarrassed state, asked Janet why she had played such a trick on him.

Janet responded, "I just wanted to test out sis's new boyfriend. I always like to take new boyfriends for a ride. Not sorry. I just wanted to make sure you were good enough for her. You passed the test okay." She then added,

"I was hoping you wouldn't. We could have had so much fun."

"Jill, why, oh why, did you not mention your sister was a twin. And equally important, that she loved to impersonate you?" David asked.

"Sorry, David, I had planned to explain about her tonight. As for you, Sis, you better know I won't forget this. I assure you; David and I will get you back for this. That I promise you," Jill said.

"Now let's all kiss and make up," Janet suggested, as David and Jill, both gave her a three- finger salute.

At that point Janet again attempted to apologize. Receiving the cold shoulder from the pair, she soon made herself scarce, saying she had another 'hot date'.

Jill tried desperately to apologize to David for Janet's actions and for not telling him earlier about her twin sister.

David couldn't resist saying, "I believe you did tell me she was older than you. Guess you failed to mention, by minutes."

They then had a good laugh at the situation and vowed revenge on Janet.

In one last, light hearted attempt to put the embarrassing episode with Janet behind him, David quipped, "You know even though I turned down Janet's offer of dessert, I would still like some dinner. Are we still eating here or going out?"

"For sure, we are having dinner here and we better get to it. I am hungry too. Since I figured you are a meat and potatoes kind of guy, I thought we would have beef tips, mashed potatoes, and salad. Does that sound ok?" Jill asked.

"Sure, that sounds great. Just tell me what I can do?" David asked.

David made the salads while Jill did the cooking. In less than an hour, the two had prepared a very nice dinner. During the dinner preparations, Jill got out a bottle of white wine from the wine cooler and said, "Bet Janet offered you red wine, didn't she?"

"Yes, your seductive sister just poured me whatever she found without even asking me. Somehow, I think you are just a might more thoughtful," he said.

"Only a might?" She laughed.

"As you by now have noticed, although we are identical twins, I feel we are surprisingly different, at least in our personalities. She is wilder than me. She drinks more, parties more, and gets herself in a lot more trouble. I do love her though, after all, she is my sister," Jill said.

They had a most delightful dinner, during which they started discussing the research they had done for their essays. They began bouncing around ideas as to where they could find out more about David's relative, Henry Mack. David told her about his research on Ancestry.com and said he had also searched Google, without any result.

They felt they should research other paintings Henry Mack might have done and, importantly, where the old mill in the painting was located. She suggested visiting art galleries that specialized in artists who painted landscapes and wildlife.

After a delightful evening, they did engage in a bit of kissing, though no dessert sex as Janet had offered. David wisely said, "You know I believe I like kissing you a little more than your sister."

She responded, "Only a little. Mister, I best not find you kissing my sister like that again."

"For sure, I will do a more thorough inspection of my kissing mate in the future to know which one of you I am kissing," he quipped.

Jill commented, "You know, Janet probably needs a good boyfriend to keep her grounded."

"I agree, too bad I don't have a twin," he joked.

4. How To Solve The Mystery/ Going To The Mountains

Initially, it was a tossup as to whether it was the challenge of solving the mystery of the paintings or the enjoyment of each other's company that bonded the couple. In any event, David and Jill began spending a great amount of time on both research and just fun stuff such as dates, travel, and getting to know each other better.

Solving the mystery consumed a fair about of their efforts. Whenever they were together, they were focused on the painting search, more than things other couples were doing. They started their quest by reviewing each other's research. What followed was the development of a plan. They each threw out their ideas and compiled a list of various leads to chase down.

They Googled listings for old grist mills in various states. As they did so, they made a list of any likely sites to perhaps visit. They also looked up books on old grist mills, taking turns reading them in public libraries or over the internet.

Jill came up with the idea of inquiring at art museums

in cities where they thought Henry might have had his paintings displayed. Along with this initiative, Jill attempted to track down other landscape painters working at the same time as Henry, to see if they had known him. This soon proved to be a dead-end. By then, most had died.

She had discovered that a nearby university had a large art program. Jill thought one of the professors there might give the pair some insight into how they might locate more of an artist's work.

Jill scored the first hit by locating another painting at a museum in Knoxville, Tennessee. The curator she spoke with, a Mister Ogle, unfortunately had very little helpful information about the painting or artist. He said the museum's work was a mountain landscape scene. Apparently, it had been anonymously donated to the museum. Mr. Ogle invited Jill to visit the museum to view the painting. Jill promised to do so at her earliest opportunity.

Her find appeared to confirm that they were searching the right geographical area. The pair were very excited, agreeing they should visit the museum. David said, "Jill, I wonder if there might be a note on the back of that one? We will have to see."

David, for his part, kept probing for any more clues from listings of Henry or Carolyn's relatives that either of them might have missed. He looked for a record of a potential marriage certificate.

Other efforts they listed to investigate included: state data bases for property ownership, obituaries, or social security records. The latter proved impossible to obtain.

The pair also quizzed their parents for any other suggestions they might have overlooked. There was a growing concern displayed by their parents that the pair was becoming obsessed with what was likely a futile effort.

The search was far from an obsession, rather it was a mutual interest and a game in which each tried to find puzzle pieces. David was quite impressed by Jill's determination and dedication to resolving the mystery of the strange notes. After a few 'work dates' in June and July, they were due a break from their weekends of research and dinners out.

"David, I can get off my job at the flower shop a couple of days the first of August. Do you think you could get away from your job for a couple of days as well? What I was thinking, we could drive up to my parent's cabin in the mountains for a long weekend. The cabin will be available for our use. What do you think?" Jill sprung her idea on David.

"Absolutely, I would really love that. It would be great to spend some time in the cooler mountain climate. We could get away from all this heat, humidity, and blasted mosquitoes."

"It will give us a break from the mill mystery for the time. However, I did locate an old mill near there that we might want to visit. Speaking of visit, it won't be too far out of the way to come back by way of Knoxville to see the painting at the museum there," she commented.

"Again, sounds like a plan," David said.

With that, the pair started making plans for their four-day weekend excursion.

"Just where in North Georgia is your parent's cabin?" David inquired.

"Oh, it's really not in North Georgia. It's in Tennessee, up in the Smoky Mountains."

"So now I see why coming back thru Knoxville makes sense. I wondered if the house was in North Georgia why we would be coming back thru Knoxville," David commented.

"Have you ever heard of Gatlinburg?" she asked him.

"Sure, I have heard of Gatlinburg. There is skiing there in winter, right?"

"Yes. Have you ever skied?" Jill asked.

"Only once, when I was in Scouts. That was up in the mountains of North Carolina. I couldn't really call that skiing though. As I recall we only tried to ski a little using that thing called a rope tow. We mainly just tubed down the slopes," David said.

"Our cabin, or mountain home, is up in the mountains above Gatlinburg in an area called Chalet Village. There are a wide assortment of homes there ranging from 'A' frames to large fancy ski lodge like affairs. Ours has four bedrooms and three and a half baths.

"Several years ago, my dad worked with the guy who built the house. Soon after he finished it, he got a job offer on the west coast. At that time the vacation home market in the area was in a decline, so the man made my dad a real good deal on the house. We rent it out part time to cover the cost.

"Our house is really neat. It has wonderful views, a great stone fireplace, and even a 'hot tub' out on the deck. I just love it there. I am sure we will have a swell time. There is everything in Gatlinburg from miniature golf, ice skating, to even an IMAX theater," Jill gushed.

"I can't wait, sounds like we can have a grand time. I am ready to go!" David said.

The pair headed out on the four-hour drive from Atlanta to Gatlinburg on a Thursday afternoon, just after lunch. Being late summer, the traffic was moderate with many families trying for one last vacation in the mountains before school started.

They had spent the two previous evenings getting provisions and packing David's SUV for the trip. The weather forecast looked swell with no hint of rain and a mild upper seventies for the mountains. "Perfect," they declared. David drove until they got to Cherokee, North Carolina, then Jill said she loved to drive over the mountains the last thirty miles, declaring, "I am an expert with the curves."

"Alright, expert, just don't damage my ride or its precious cargo," David said.

Jill had already proved to be a safe driver so he really had great confidence in her ability to navigate the mountain road. It took them nearly an hour to cover the last thirty miles to Gatlinburg. After entering Great Smokey Mountain National Park, the road began to twist as they gained elevation. Soon the scenery became more striking, with the distant vistas. They stopped at the parking lot at the Clingmans Dome pass to take numerous pictures.

As they approached the edge of town, Jill asked if he wanted to go directly to the cabin or drive through town first. David gathered she would like to go to the cabin first so that was his suggestion.

"Wow, this is some cabin. Not so little. Quite impressive," David announced as Jill parked in front of the two story Swiss contemporary chalet. The house was clad in cedar siding with a multitude of decks and a massive stone chimney. The house was situated on a knoll of land with three-hundred-degree views of the mountains below and the distance hills to the west.

"Come on, I'll show you inside," Jill said, while unlocking the front door. "We can come back to get our stuff."

The home's interior walls were clad in smooth cedar siding, giving the home a warm aroma of cedar. From the entry there was a large modern kitchen to the left and a dining room to the right. The main feature was a giant great room / conversation pit with a large stone fireplace and a towering two-story chimney. The area above the conversation pit was open to the ceiling and skylight two floors overhead.

Behind the entry wall was a stairwell with stairs to the lower level as well as stairs to the second floor. Rounding out the main floor was a wet bar behind the kitchen. Jill then led David upstairs where there were three more bedrooms and two baths. Two of the bedrooms had their own balconies.

"What is this? Fieldstone in the shower? And a skylight," David said, quite astonished.

"Yep, the guy who designed it had some unusual ideas," Jill commented. "Come along, the best of the house awaits," she announced.

They went back down the stairs to the main level. "I want to go out on the deck and see the view," he said.

"Oh, we shall, but first let me show you the downstairs."

As they made their way down, she commented, "The master bedroom is down there. It is the room my parents usually get, but you know, they are not here," she said with a big grin.

At the bottom of the stairs was a hall leading to a game room and laundry. She then opened the other door.

"Oh, my goodness, look at this, the room has its own little stone fireplace! and…is this huge bed a waterbed?" he asked.

"Sure is. And in here we have the master bath with a large sauna."

Walking back into the bedroom, they passed the large sliding glass door with an inviting patio outside.

"Now let me show you my favorite part of the house," she said.

With that she led him back into the master bedroom and over to a small door beside the stone fireplace. He noticed her flick a switch on the wall before unlocking the door.

Hearing a noise, David asked, "What is that?"

She instructed him to follow her. Then she opened the door and there was a metal spiral stair leading upward. Entering the stairwell, it was suddenly cooler.

"Oh, it's the hot tub and it is bubbling away. That was the sound. This room, it's all glass and look at that view, unbelievable. I am ready to get in, how about you?" David asked.

"I think perhaps we should unload first, besides the spa will need to heat up for about an hour," she commented.

"This place is just, so over the top. You called this a mere mountain cabin. I can certainly see why your parents like it up here so well."

The pair unloaded the mountain of supplies they had brought with them. They had food, mainly snack stuff, however they also had made off with a couple of bottles of wine from their parents' supply. Then there were the DVDs of some of Jill's favorite movies she planned to play for David.

"Let's talk dinner tonight. Though it is only 4:30 we probably should go down to town soon and be at the restaurant by 5:30 since all the restaurants get crowded with tourists after that. I thought tonight I would take you to my favorite 'The Open Hearth'. I think you will really like it. Tomorrow night can be your treat," Jill said.

"Do we have time for a snack and a glass of wine before we go?" David asked. "I want to just sit out on that deck and take in the view," he said.

"Sure, great idea, I'll get the cheese and crackers. You pour us a little wine," Jill offered.

As David was getting the bottle of wine out of Jill's cooler, he made a discovery. Amongst two bottles of white wine was a bottle of champagne. Never having had champagne, he was intrigued. *That is supposed to be for special occasions, he thought. His mind then went off in an erotic direction involving Jill and the hot tub.* Moving on, he gathered wine glasses and poured the wine.

"This view is to die for," he said as they watched the afternoon sun getting lower on the horizon. "I could get used to this. So, Jill, have you brought a lot of guys up here?" David asked.

"No, you are the first, without my parents chaperoning," she said. "Now as for my scandalous sister, there is not much telling. She is such an embarrassment, you know. But at other times she can be sweet."

Soon the pair headed back down the twisting mountain road toward the park end of town. David was now driving and Jill providing commentary and directions.

"I think we will get our dinner at the 'Open Hearth' then I will take you on a brief walking tour of the town," she said.

"That sounds like a great idea," David responded.

He recognized the pleasure she seemed to be having showing off everything to him. Whenever he looked at her, she had her infectious smile. "Jill, I believe you are the happiest person I have ever met. You are always smiling."

That comment caused her to blush. She responded, "Have you thought that may have something to do with you?"

With that comment, David bent over and gave her a gentle kiss.

As they were discussing the entrees, she told him that the prime rib was really good there, and so he went with that. She joined him in that selection. He agreed the meal was excellent. Normally the two refrained from desserts, but tonight she insisted they share a large chocolate concoction with ice cream.

"We sure need to do some walking after such a big meal," he remarked. "It was really terrific. I only hope the place you have picked out for me to take you tomorrow night is as good."

"Don't worry, it will be. We will leave Gatlinburg fat as pigs," she responded.

As they walked along, there was an unending string of shops and eateries. There was also a mass of people clogging the sidewalks.

"What is that?" David asked.

"Oh, you mean the 'Gondola Lift'. That is on the menu. The lift takes about one hundred people at a time up the three miles to the ski lodge. Obviously, we won't be able to ski now, but ice skating? Well yes! I must see you on skates," she joked.

"You must surely be trying to kill me," David commented.

They neared the end of what Jill called 'the main drag' (the main street through town). Jill announced, "This is where I suggest we eat tomorrow night." The building was an old log cabin establishment with the name, 'The Pioneer Restaurant'.

"Looks interesting, we will do that."

They arrived back at 'Windover' (the name of her parent's cabin) about seven thirty, just as the sun was starting to set.

Jill said, "Come on let's watch the sunset from the spa. It will be grand."

"Well, don't you know you can't go swimming right after a big meal. I might drown," David again joked.

"I suspect I might be able to save you. Though I might have to give you mouth to mouth," she mused.

"I may just drown, if that is the case" he joined in with more silliness. "Let me go and get my swimming trunks. I will be right back."

"Really!" she said giving David a sly look, while taking his hand.

She proceeded to lead him down to the master bedroom, gather a handful of towels, and start to disrobe. She encouraged him to do likewise. Somewhat embarrassed, yet quite excited at the same time, he obliged, concealing his nakedness with a towel.

"Oh, almost forgot the bubbly," she said, "You go ahead and get in I will be right there."

The water felt delicious as he sank into it. While the hot water felt wonderfully relaxing, at the same time he was becoming nervous over what he was pretty sure was going to take place shortly. Soon Jill returned with a bottle of champagne in a bucket of ice. Setting it down within reach of the spa, she proceeded to modestly drop her towel and give David a quick glimpse of her fully naked. With shaky hands, he managed to finally pop the champagne cork and pour some into the glasses.

From then on it was a really fantastic experience.

An hour later two well done and completely exhausted human lobsters emerged.

David commented, "Dear, you may need to help me downstairs to shower. I fear I may be too weak to move."

"Oh, come on, you are a young man in his prime. A little exercise shouldn't hurt you," she mused. "Besides, you still have to build us a fire in the fireplace downstairs."

"A fire as boiled as we are. Are you insane?"

"Oh yes, it will provide a romantic setting for our first night sleeping together."

"Yes, ma'am!" he weakly agreed.

"Say you aren't a bad snorer, are you?" she asked.

"No, I don't think so."

As they lay in bed that night, David commented, "Even if we never find that old mill or solve the mystery of the paintings, I want you to know, finding you, that was the miracle for me."

"That is so sweet of you. I feel the same. Maybe that was the purpose of the paintings, to bring two people together," she said.

"Could be," he agreed.

With that they fell asleep in each other's arms as the embers of the small fire gave up their glow.

Awakening the following morning, David greeted Jill, "Good morning, my cuddly bed mate. Did I snore too bad?"

"No, not so bad. I only had to kick you once to tone you down," she responded.

"Say, what's on our agenda for today, Love?"

"Well, for starters, I thought we might go down to the Village where there is a great waffle place. Then I wanted you to ride the Gondola up to the ski area to check that out. I thought we might picnic for lunch in the park, then go ice skating late this afternoon."

"I see. Well, you do have the day pretty well planned. Good idea putting off ice skating till this afternoon. We can have fun before I injure myself." He added, "Let's get to it. Me be hungry."

Just as Jill had predicted The Waffle Place was great. In addition to wonderful strawberry waffles, they had fresh squeezed orange juice in tall frosted beer mugs. When they finished stuffing themselves, it was almost 10 o'clock.

"Gondola time," Jill piped up.

For David's first time going up to the ski lodge and skating rink, Jill decided they must ride the Gondola Lift up from Gatlinburg. This would give him a good bird's eye view of the town, Chalet Village, and the mountains. While riding the lift didn't make him nervous, the ice skating did. The placard next to the gondola car door said the capacity was 120. Fortunately, it wasn't that full, with only about twenty adults and a good many noisy kids.

As the car lurched with the start upward, it rapidly picked up speed. The kid's shrieks accelerated right along with the speed of the car. Jill and David laughed at the excited little ones. It was amazing when the gondola got up to Chalet Village. It went almost over the top of some of the cabins. Jill told him that she had heard stories of problems with privacy. The cabin occupants apparently didn't like seeing onlookers zooming above their homes.

The mountain views to the east were spectacular. They had picked a great day for their excursion. The few puffy clouds that painted the sky, cast shadows over the mountainous terrain of the forest, interrupted with only a few meandering roads. The town slowly disappeared. There was a disconcerting clicking and mild jarring as the car rode over the various support tower rollers.

The car slowed as it came into the upper station, stopping very smoothly. Disembarking, the pair made their way to view the ski lodge and to explore the area.

Looking up at the now grassy ski slopes, David asked Jill which ones she had skied down. Her response un-nerved him. She said practically all. After their brief sightseeing at the lodge, the pair rode the gondola back to town, picked up David's SUV, and returned to the house. By then it was 1 o'clock and they decided to just picnic out on the deck.

Jill sensed that David was nervous about ice skating, but she had a solution. Her solution was to get David slightly drunk before taking to the ice. She felt that would relax him and would dull the pain when he hit the ice. As one might guess, she had received that tip from sister Janet.

"You know, David, I would like to drive us up to the ski lodge. Why don't you have a couple of glasses of wine to re-lax you before skating. I feel it will help you," Jill suggested.

"If you say so, I am always open to suggestions," he responded.

With that, Jill plied him with wine until he was relaxed, but could still walk.

David had never ice skated and only roller skated once. Jill, on the other hand had ice skated up at the ski lodge on several occasions. Jill drove the pair up to the lodge parking lot. Upon arriving there, Jill then led David to the large enclosed ice-skating pavilion. They gave the skate rental attendant their shoe sizes and he handed them skates. Then they proceeded with the arduous lacing of their skates. Soon they were on the ice.

She was remarkably good. David was sure he would embarrass both of them and would most likely get hurt. The wine he had consumed, proved to do the trick. He became relaxed on the ice despite several falls, a couple in which he took her down with him. She took that in stride. In all it was a great fun experience for both. They declared it would not be their last time skating.

Over their four days, the two enjoyed all that Gatlinburg had to offer. He beat her playing miniature golf. She far outlasted him with shopping, as one might have expected. Despite all David's concerns, neither got hurt ice skating.

All in all, the long weekend could not have gone better. Both acknowledged how much they hated that it had to end. As David said, all good things must end, but they could also begin with a twinkle.

The pair did go back by way of Knoxville to see Henry's painting in the museum there. It was a lovely scene of another tumbling mountain stream with trees in full fall color. Mr. Ogle was even kind enough to take the painting down to see if there was any strange note on the back. Regrettably, there wasn't.

What the pair failed to do was visit any grist mills. More time for that later they agreed.

5. Back To School – Holidays & Skiing

It was to be a big school year for both David and Jill. They were each entering their sophomore year and both had elected to redefine their courses of study. David had elected to give up Civil Engineering for Construction Management. He had a desire to create buildings and things more exciting than infrastructure such as dams, bridges, or utilities. He didn't care if it was houses or commercial buildings, he just wanted to build.

Jill, on the other hand, decided on a degree in education with an emphasis on art and history. The research she had been doing on paintings and old mills had helped with her decision. Another big change for Jill this year would be sharing an off-campus rental house with two other girls. She had introduced one roommate, Diana, to David, but he was yet to meet her other roommate.

In addition to her roommates, Jill also had quite a few female friends. As for David, Bill and John were about it for close male friends. In David's case, he was too busy with school for a great amount of partying. Then also,

Jill and the old mill hunt took most of any spare time he had.

A lot of their friends failed to understand the strange story of how the two met or about their search for the elusive old mill. People thought the mill search was sort of weird. As a result, the pair seldom mentioned it.

In late September, when the football team had an away game, Jill and her roommates decided to have a small party at their new apartment. Jill told David that the party was to introduce Beth to some eligible guys, since she was without a boyfriend. John had a steady girlfriend, but despite that, he was always looking. Bill was without a girlfriend at present and readily accepted the party invite.

The party was a lot of fun, even in the absence of alcohol. The girls had a variety of snacks, both those they made and store bought. They also played a number of pair's games. David surprised the group by excelling in charades. It turned out that the party accomplished the goal. Bill and Beth hit it off very well. This introduced Bill into Jill's group. John and his girlfriend mixed in frequently as well. Soon the group took on the name 'The Six Pack' and became their own clique.

One of the next events after the girls' party was a football game at Tech. John was going to school there and arranged to get them student tickets. Since alcohol was not allowed to be brought in to the stadium, it was always a challenge to smuggle it in. Rum and coke had long been a staple at the games.

The group implored various guises to get some into the stadium. Jill opted for a small flask in her bra. David liked her idea but said he was not properly equipped to use that trick. He chose slipping a couple of flasks in a hollowed-out stadium seat cushion. Others in the group came up with their own solutions. Amazingly they all escaped capture by the alcohol police and a grand time was had by all, despite Tech losing badly.

Thanksgiving rolled around, but it provided only three days off from classes, so any extended travel to visit mill sites, was not possible. David and Jill were spending the time with their families. Jill was invited to eat Thanksgiving dinner with David's folks and likewise David was invited to dine with Jill's family. David took pleasure in kidding her about his putting on pounds with two huge meals back-to-back.

"You know, both the dinner at your folks and that at mine were grand but, did you notice the different dishes and traditions. My mother had dressing without oysters and yours with. In my family, the men carve the turkey. In yours, the women do. What is with that? Why doesn't your dad carve?" David asked.

"I don't know, that's just how we do it. Do those things bother you?" she asked.

"No, not at all. I suppose each of us could learn to try new foods and ways of serving it, don't you think?"

"Sure do, and my family doesn't have pecan pie and your mother's is to die for," Jill commented.

"Isn't it, though."

"You know we both gobbled till we wobbled."

"You more than me, mister."

It was a joyous time for all.

While having dinner at her house, Jill's folks invited David to join them for Christmas in Gatlinburg. They said he could come up after he celebrated the holiday with his folks. Even more interesting than that, her parents said they were going to be in Gatlinburg for only one week and he and Jill could use the house for a party with their friends between Christmas and New Year's. "Wow, that is great!" Jill thanked them as did David, saying how nice that was of them. David promised he would see to it that no damage was done.

Soon after Thanksgiving, Jill and David began planning for a grand party at the mountain house. The party was to be right before and including New Year's Eve. As for guests, Jill's two roommates and their boyfriends were a given. Then there was Janet. Somehow Jill felt they should invite her and whatever boyfriend she had at the time. Though reluctant to do so, they agreed it was the right thing to do.

As it turned out, shortly after the Thanksgiving dinner with Jill's parent's, plans changed somewhat. The Gatlinburg party was still on but, as it turned out, her parents would not be spending Christmas in the mountains after all. It seemed Jill's parents church was producing an event called The Singing Christmas Tree. Somewhat surprisingly, Janet wanted to participate in the week-long event culminating on Christmas eve. She was to be one of the thirty-five singers on the tree.

David or Jill had never heard of the event. Apparently, a large artificial tree was built of special scaffolding then decorated to look like a giant tree with lights. The singers, mainly the church choir members would make their way to various places within the tree concealed except for their upper bodies. They and the audience would then sing Christmas Carols.

This event sounded interesting to the pair. Jill's parents even gave David's parents tickets to the concert. Since both families would now be in town for Christmas, David was again invited over to Jill's house for Christmas.

For both families, Christmas was celebrated with decorations, food, and parties. The kick- off was picking out Christmas trees. David discovered Jill loved to shop for trees. No artificial tree would do for either family. David also was to learn that his girlfriend was most particular when it came to her tree. Patience was the rule of those who participated with her in tree shopping.

David joined Jill in shopping for her parent's tree and she joined his parents and him in the same event. Decorating the trees with Jill was also an enlightening event for David as well. His family had old traditional lights and ornaments while the Howard's had newer lighting and some rather peculiar ornaments. David was also to learn about Jill's practice of collecting Christmas ornaments everywhere she visited. *He must remember not to speak negatively about any of her ornaments, he thought.*

The Howard's were big on entertaining, so they usually hosted a big party for family, friends, and neighbors a week before Christmas. Again, David and his parents were invited. It was quite a party with great food with eggnog and champagne served for young and old alike.

Christmas Eve everyone joined the large crowd at the

Howard's church for the Singing Christmas Tree performance. It was unlike anything David or Jill had ever seen. It was truly a heart-warming experience. The audience, including David and Jill, joined in singing many Christmas Carols. Jill said her favorite was *White Christmas* while David said *Silver Bells* was his.

Both sets of parents held package opening on Christmas morning with a grand feast at noon on Christmas day.

For Christmas, Santa Claus presented David with an Apple I-watch, while Santa did Jill one better with a new Apple Mac Book Air computer. As for the couple's gift exchange, David gave Jill a quite nice emerald necklace. She in turn gave him a leather coat.

Quickly the excitement of their first Christmas together turned to the excitement of their first big party in Gatlinburg. The two spent the day after Christmas packing David's SUV for the trip to the mountains. They planned to take off for Gatlinburg early on the morning of December 27th. The rest of the guests, including Janet and her boyfriend would arrive on the 28th.

With a solemn promise to stay at the house and not to drive after drinking, Jill's parents had agreed to provide the couple some beer and wine for their party. Jill and David thanked them for their trust.

On the drive up, the two discussed the favorite times at Christmas and told each other of their past Christmases. For both, they agreed it was their favorite Holiday, not just because of all the parties and festivities, but because of the event that Christmas stood for. The pair like too many young people their age, had not attended church regularly since they entered college. Their primary attendance was at Christmas and Easter. Both agreed they must do better with their attendance in the coming year. Jill joked she would convert David to a Baptist while David vowed to bring her over to being a Methodist.

Their conversation then turned to the weather forecast for the mountains. David had been checking it the past couple of days and it seemed the prospect of snow had crept into the forecast.

"Jill, what do you think about the weather? You do know there is a forecast of snow for New Year's Eve," David said, quite excitedly.

"No! You don't really think it will snow do you? Wouldn't it be great to get snowed in," Jill gushed.

"Well, if it were just you and me, getting snowed in it would be swell, but with a whole house full and your trouble making sister Janet, I think it may get a bit challenging," he commented.

It appeared the stars were to align and a significant snowfall was forecast to begin late on the 29th. The party goers rushed to arrive before the snow began. David worried what would happen if they did get snowed in on the mountain. He felt too much snow might have them confined to the house.

While Jill failed to share David's concerns about being snowbound, she and David did make sure the house was well stocked with food and drink. She also pointed out that they had an assortment of games for indoors as well as numerous CDs and DVDs.

While discussing the pros and cons of a big snow, Jill mentioned all the fun things the group could do, such as sledding, tubing, and skiing.

"But you can ski, I can't, and I suspect most of the others can't either. We will likely get broken limbs." He then added, "Let it snow! Let it snow! Let it snow!"

The first couple to arrive was Bill and Beth. Neither had been to the house before, or for that matter Gatlinburg.

"My, what a place," was Bill's greeting when Jill answered the door.

"Jill, I have heard you mention your parent's cabin here but I had no idea it was this grand," Beth commented as Jill and David showed the pair around.

Jill, with David's help, had come up with a plan on how to distribute the bedrooms. After subtracting the master bedroom, which they claimed for themselves, they would have each couple draw bedroom names from a bowl as they arrived. Jill quickly overruled David's idea of each individual drawing for who they would be paired up with.

Soon thereafter, John and Diana arrived, followed by Janet and her latest boyfriend Ron. By six that evening everyone had arrived. David had been glued to the Weather Channel on his cell phone for most of the day tracking the changing forecast. For someone who loved snow but had experienced little of it while living in Atlanta, he was beside himself about the snow.

Everyone was overly excited with the prospect of a major snowfall. With the forecast for the snow to start around nine that evening, the group piled into two vehicles and headed downtown to the 'Open Hearth Restaurant'. They felt that might be their only good restaurant meal option for days.

Dinner conversation that evening centered on activities the group might enjoy. A survey was taken of who had skiing experience. It was determined that only Jill, Janet, and John had ever skied. David did not count himself as having ever skied. The others, though never having been on skis or snow boards, were game to try. So, it was decided that at the earliest opportunity they would get to the ski lodge, rent skis, and have a go at that.

David, having been a good boy scout and had practiced their motto always, 'Be Prepared', had brought along chains for his four-wheeled drive SUV and felt he could shuttle everyone the short distance up to the ski lodge.

The group arrived back at the 'Windover' house just as the first snowflakes began falling at eight o'clock. David and Jill served up some wine and she put on some music. Bill undertook putting more wood on the coals in the fireplace. Everyone was mellowing out nicely.

Janet announced, "Hay gang, Ron and I are hitting the hot tub. Grab your birthday suits and come join us."

"Janet, No! No nude bathing in the hot tub. We told everyone to bring suits," Jill announced.

Beth piped up with, "Not drunk enough for nude bathing yet?"

With those remarks, Janet responded, "Well Ron, guess we will have to hot tub after these prudes go to bed."

Jill then commented, "With the snow falling, the spa room out on the deck, would be a grand place to watch it fall. How about it, David, and other properly clothed one's care to join me?"

With that invitation, the six, 'non-nudists' changed into swimming attire. David turned on the outside lights and everyone ran out onto the deck through the snow to the steaming spa. It turned out to be a grand place to watch the falling snow. The stone wall of the massive chimney formed the back wall of the large round spa enclosure. Floor to roof windows formed the other one-hundred- eighty -degrees of the semicircular room. They had a perfect view of the snow.

As their wine and the bubbling waters soaked away their cares, the craziness began.

David led off with, "This is grand, but I believe I am going to open the door, go out on the deck and build a snowman! I suspect it won't be too long before I will return as a snowman myself."

"Great idea, let's go out in pairs with each pair building a small snowman," Jill suggested.

Everyone agreed that was a splendid idea. And so, dressed only in their swimming suits, each pair braved the snow on their bare feet and bodies. It was amazing how quickly they completed their tiny snowmen before running back to jump in the luscious steaming waters.

The last pair, John and Diana, was declared to have fashioned the most appealing little snowman. All agreed that they had the advantage of having observed the techniques and failures of the others to gain the advantage with their creation.

After a late night watching a movie on the big screen over the fireplace, the group finally called it a night.

David and Jill were the first to stir the next morning. After dressing, they rushed out to begin playing in the snow. David measured it to be six inches, a whole lot to a Georgia boy. Soon the pair had dug out the two sleds stored in the basement and were putting them to good use on the hill outside the house. Of course, they frequently pelted each other with a good wet snowball or two.

It wasn't too long before the others began joining them in the snow, that was except for Janet and Ron.

Jill jokingly commented, "David, do go check the spa to make sure they are not still boiling away."

With only two sleds, the group took turns with them while the others engaged in pelting them with snowballs.

Since by then it was almost lunch time, the girls, including Janet, went in to prepare lunch for all. The guys created a blazing fire in the fireplace and took care of the music. While feeding their appetites, the group discussed the possibility of being able to get to the ski lodge for some tubing and skiing. Jill suggested ice skating but only David took to that idea. David said he would put on his chains and test the road right after lunch.

The test run went well. It seemed that the main road leading up to the lodge had already received some attention from a snowplow. The side roads such as theirs were manageable with his chains. Six of the group piled into David's SUV and headed up to the lodge. Janet and Ron stayed behind for more of their private fun and games. Ron said he felt his vehicle could make it up to the lodge and they would be up there shortly.

Amongst the group, only Jill and John had much experience with skiing.

"Come on, David, you can do this. Look, Diana hasn't skied before and she is going to go with John. I will help you learn," Jill implored him.

"Ok, you will be the cause of my demise, I just want you to know that," David moaned.

Meanwhile Bill and Beth chose tubing down a separate slope next to the main ski runs. David longingly eyed that activity and gained a promise from Jill to try that once they did the skiing thing for a little while.

Despite his reluctance, David got his snowplow technique down pretty quickly. Jill showed off by zipping by him when he fell, spraying him with snow from her skis. In all, the group spent a fun filled three hours on the slopes. As promised, Jill and David did try the tubing. In that activity they came the closest to disaster, when Jill on her tube crashed into David, sending them both tumbling out of control down the slope.

New Year's Eve was quite memorable. They had another three inches of snow to recoat everything. David, Jill, John, and Diana celebrated it in the spa watching the snow and sipping champagne. The champagne bottles were kept chilled in the fresh snow out on the deck. A designated 'hot tubber' would go and retrieve one when it was required.

The other four had become too drunk, too early, to be even able to walk. Jill commented she wasn't surprised by Janet, but she was by Beth and Bill.

By noon on New Year's Day, the sun was out and the snow was receding from the roads as the group commenced their departure. David and Jill were the last to leave, having to attempt to do some preliminary cleanup so that the cleaning service wouldn't be overwhelmed.

"You know, that was a pretty great party," David commented.

"Yep, I certainly agree. What made it special to me though is having the best partner with me," Jill said.

"That is so sweet of you," David said as he leaned over and kissed her. David then quipped, "but you know, I believe Ron got more bed time with your twin than I got with you."

"You men are all pigs. That's all you think of" she responded, in jest.

6. The Twin Strikes Again

It was to be a big summer. The summer before their junior year of college. The past year had been busy for both David and Jill. They had both changed or settled on their course of studies for their degrees and in doing so had to put in extra work to insure they would graduate on schedule. There had been little time to focus on the Old Mill Quest.

With the start of summer, they were looking forward to not only new, more exciting summer jobs, but the opportunity for a bit more time together. David, having chosen a degree in Construction Management had a job as an intern for a small construction company. Jill on the other hand was going to be a camp counselor at a nearby summer camp. All looked great.

Well, we need to back up a moment and catch up with the black sheep, twin Janet. She too was progressing with her efforts for a degree in music from a college in Virginia. Unlike her sister Jill, she had met a young man, who, like too many of her boyfriends, was not too grounded. Jeff had dropped out of college and had started a band a semester earlier. He was planning to take the band on the road and if successful, not return to school.

Jeff had convinced Janet to join the band as a singer and electric piano player. Jill's folks were flipping out over that prospect. They were at the point of threatening to disown her if she didn't continue her college studies.

By the end of May, Janet had been practicing with the band and performing at local engagements for a couple of months. Their group was slated to start a Midwest tour in June.

The first of May, Janet sent Jill a video tape of one of the bands performances with an ominous note. The note encouraged Jill to practice some of her songs. Needless to say, this raised a red flag for Jill. She did not tell her parents about the note. About a week later, Janet called Jill and sprung her great plan.

What she disclosed to Jill was; she had been having a problem with one of her wisdom teeth. Her dentist recommended having all of them removed. As if having oral surgery was not enough, she had the terrific idea of having her tonsils removed at the same time. She felt that would minimize the likelihood of a throat infection from her singing. Adding more craziness to the situation, she wanted Jill to take her place and fill in for her as a singer in the band for about a week. That was all the time she thought she would be away from singing with the band.

"You absolutely must be kidding," David responded, laughing at the insanity of the idea.

"No, she is quite serious," Jill commented.

"Oh, knowing her I can believe that. You are not really considering it? Are you?"

"And does that mean you will fill in sleeping with her boyfriend as well?" he joked.

"Absolutely not. How could you say such a thing!"

"Just kidding!" David said. "Are you really sure she is your sister. I mean you are so considerate and level headed and she, well she is just so different to put it politely. I thought twins were totally alike."

"Oh, apparently they are booked into a spot there in Virginia near DC for the next four weeks. After that, they are going to tour across the US with another larger band until Fall. She is having a fit for me, and you, to come up and see them perform. What do you think? Perhaps we could do our end of semester classes celebration in Virginia. Have you ever been there? Maybe we could check out old mills in the area, you reckon?" she asked.

Much to David's chagrin, Jill started practicing Janet's songs and, in the end, agreed to fill in for her one week. Needless to say, her parents were quite distressed about the whole thing.

Joking, Jill told David, "I will try and find some old mills to visit on my travels through Kentucky with the band."

"You had better not be there that long," David exclaimed.

"David, I want you to come up to Virginia for my first concert with the band. Do you think you might be able to?" she pleaded.

"I'll do better than that, I will drive you up there. I wouldn't want to miss her boyfriend's first encounter with you. You know if your sister hasn't told him yet about you, it might be a great opportunity to prank her real good.

Also, since Janet said she was just 'testing me out' for you, perhaps you could do the same for her in a way," David suggested.

"What are you thinking?" Jill asked.

"Well, how about this: We show up a day earlier than expected, you dress up as her, pretend to be her, show up late for rehearsal and tell Jeff the reason you were late was you were having morning sickness," David suggested.

"Oh my! That is really a bold plan. She might actually do me harm if I were to pull that on her and Jeff," Jill warned.

"It would be interesting to see how Jeff might react though, don't you think?"

"Yah, but it might break them up and really hurt Janet."

David commented, "That's true, but I suspect from what you have told me, Jeff is just using her and she is about to make a bad mistake dropping out of school for him."

"As always, you are probably right, and if they truly love each other, then they will still be together, that is after they have killed us!" she joked.

With that, the two set about making travel plans for the 'State for Lovers' as the license plates read. At the same time as David was researching hotels in the vicinity, Jill set about doing research on old mill sites they could visit in the Appalachian Mountains area. Jill was still very much engaged in her painting search for old mills.

Once Jill had decided to oblige Janet and fill in for her, she asked if she would hold off telling Jeff until she got up there and auditioned. Janet agreed. With that, she and David set about planning their prank on Janet. Their plan was to show up in Virginia a day earlier than she told Janet they would be arriving.

David's map showed it to be slightly less than five hundred miles from Atlanta to Washington D.C. He felt that was too far for one day's trip. He decided they would break the trip up with an overnight in Roanoke, Virginia. Then the next day on to Falls Church, where the band was to be performing. David had lined up a nice Best Western hotel there for three nights.

Jill had read about an old mill near Luray, Virginia, a place about eighty miles away that she wanted them to visit if they had the time.

On the drive up to Virginia, the pair refined their plans. First, they would need to verify with Janet that she had not told Jeff that Jill was coming up to fill in. Second, they would need to confirm the time the band would be rehearsing and also where the rehearsal would be the next morning. Finally, they would need to find a way to ensure that Janet was at least an hour late for rehearsal.

As the confident one, David said, "Piece of cake."

"Oh, you really think so. Answer me these questions…how do you think I can get hold of her costume? And more important, how can we keep her away for an hour?" Jill asked.

"Well, the costume shouldn't be an issue since it is only a rehearsal. Just try and dress like you think she would. I agree, keeping her away will be more difficult. Let's try this. Your sister likes to drink. Why don't we get her drunk the night before, change the time on her watch for an hour later. Or I could offer to pick her up and drive her over to the rehearsal," he suggested.

The plan the two settled on was a combination of getting her drunk that night, changing her alarm clock, and then David calling her the next morning after she realized her car wouldn't start, thanks to David's handiwork. Crazy as it sounded, that was their plan.

Then came the part of Jill pretending to be Janet at the rehearsal that morning. She was very nervous. David kept telling her to relax and lighten up. David was to enter the rehearsal first pretending to be a 'roadie' from the larger band that Jeff's band would be traveling with. In about fifteen minutes, Jill was to come in. She would do her bit by apologizing to Jeff about being late. She was to tell him she thought she had morning sickness. All the time, David would try his best to surreptitiously film Jeff's response.

"Who are you and what are you doing here? This is a closed rehearsal," one of the band members told David.

"Yah man. I understand, I'm a 'roadie' with George's band and will be traveling to gigs with you all. Just wanted to see your act if I could," David explained.

By that time, Jeff had come forward and gave his ok for David to stay. Soon the big moment arrived as a slightly disheveled 'Janet,' or Jill pretending to be her, entered and Jeff took her aside to question her tardy arrival.

"Well Jeffie, sorry to be a little late. It's just that I think I have a touch of morning sickness this morning."

"What the hell! Are you saying you are pregnant? Now at this time? What happened? I thought you were safe?" Jeff went on and on.

It was all of what David had expected and more. He felt sick for Janet. David caught it all on video. Meanwhile, David called Janet and offered to run over and pick her up. He hated leaving Jill to ad lib with Jeff. In about fifteen minutes, David was back with Janet. Once again David attempted to capture on video the scene that played out when Jeff saw the real Janet and asked who the imposter was and then if she was pregnant.

After a great deal of discussion between Jeff, Janet, David, and Jill, the band finally did a brief rehearsal with Jill doing quite a good job singing some of Janet's songs. When lunch time rolled around, Jeff and Janet went to lunch alone to sort out the effects of the joke. Before lunch, they suggested the four of them have dinner together that night. It would be their only chance since the band would be playing the next night and then again Saturday.

At dinner that night, fortunately all was forgiven and Jeff had taken the surprise and prank in stride. David and Jill did not show Janet the video or let Jeff know his outburst had been filmed.

Janet had told Jeff about Jill filling in for her for a week and he said that would be fine. Jeff even suggested that both of them perform the next two nights, saying the audience would love seeing twins. Surprising to David, Jill agreed to do that. They asked David to video their set for their parents.

David asked Jill, "Aren't you afraid how your parents will react to seeing this. I mean they are already upset about Janet, now seeing you too, they may be livid."

"Oh, I hope not. You don't really think so, do you?"

"Hopefully not, but please, if they are, tell them I had nothing to do with it," David said. "By the way, I will attempt to explain to your parents that you promised me to come straight back home after one week with the band."

Janet's dental work was to take place on Tuesday, then her tonsils on Friday. Janet assured Jeff that she would be able to resume performing the following week. David and Jill really didn't believe her doctor would agree to do tonsils surgery so soon after tooth extractions. Unfortunately, they were wrong. He did do the surgery.

The pair made a brief excursion to Luray to see that mill. Unfortunately, though a quite scenic old mill, it was not the one they had been searching for. David departed back to Atlanta for his summer job.

As might have been predicted, Janet was to come down with an infection from her surgeries. No sooner had David arrived back home than he got a frantic call from Jill. It seemed Janet had come up with a bad infection in her mouth and would be out longer. Jill said it was so bad that their mother was coming up to take care of her. Jeff was begging Jill to stay and continue with the band. Jill had, reluctantly, agreed to only one additional week, period.

"David, you are right. I really don't feel like Janet and I are twins. You will never believe what she did. Her oral surgeon gave her two medications after her extractions, a pain killer and an antibiotic. She took the pain medication, but after reading on the antibiotic label that alcohol was not to be taken with it, she chose drinking over taking the antibiotic. Can you imagine anything so very dumb?" Jill said.

"Jill, you and your mother really need to have an intervention with Janet. That girl is heading for trouble with Jeff, the band thing, and drinking. She needs to find a stable boyfriend and give up the alcohol while she still can. She is too pretty and sweet and perhaps, intelligent, to throw everything away. Convince her to stay in school," he added.

"I wholeheartedly agree. My mother and I will really work on that," Jill committed.

Finally, a week later than she originally planned, Jill flew back into Atlanta. David was there to pick her up. She said that Janet had improved and she had committed to being back in school in the fall. She had also promised to give up drinking except a little on special occasions. David's take on it was, 'Time will tell…'

Back in Atlanta, the pair attempted to reclaim what remained of their summer plans. David was working in an intern job with a construction company while Jill was still able to start her camp counselor job at a camp about an hour from Atlanta. Their jobs, not to mention Jill being over an hour away, took a toll on their dating life. He was able to get up to her camp on two occasions. At those times, she snuck away for a day each visit. During these brief visits, they explored small towns and eateries in north Georgia. And oh yes, looked for lost old mills.

Jill, for her part was really enjoying working with the younger kids. She felt it was good experience for her now chosen career in education. David also was getting into his chosen line of work with his summer job. He was put in charge of two homes for a local builder. He too was gaining valuable experience and excelled in the job.

The summer was far too short. Before they returned to

classes the first of September, the pair again borrowed Jill's parents vacation home for another get-away. This time in lieu of going alone, they invited another couple along. Unfortunately, the couple they had invited canceled out at the last minute so again they ventured to Gatlinburg alone.

As David told Jill, "I am never alone when I am with you and I would prefer it to be just the two of us."

On this trip, the pair finally had the opportunity to do a bit of the hiking that David so enjoyed, and yes, they even visited a couple of old mills that Jill had located. Again, neither mill matched that in Henry's paintings.

As for the hiking, David had bought both he and Jill day packs. He had also bought a small collapsible cooler. They packed their picnic lunches and soft drinks in their backpacks and hit the trails. To David's great pleasure, it seemed that Jill was quite at home on the trail. They both committed to more such excursions in the future.

7. Another Painting

Jill was quite excited to be taking an art class as an elective that year in school. She was very impressed with her instructor, Ms. Burns. Apparently so were the half a dozen guys in the class. They were obviously taken with her youthfulness and uncommon beauty. Ms. Burns had each student in the relatively small class, tell a bit about what had led them to become interested in art and in taking her class. At that point one overzealous, and yes stupid guy answered, "I just like taking classes with pretty professors." Ms. Burns did not laugh.

"Mr. Jacobs while I commend your candor, I do believe you will find you have made a mistake signing up for my class," the instructor responded.

Jill, when it was her turn, mentioned the two Old Mill paintings. Ms. Burns seemed intrigued and asked Jill to meet with her after class. She gave Jill a tip on where she might look to find more paintings by her artist.

Ms. Burns suggested that Jill should check out art galleries in tourist areas where scenic artists sold their works. She said that many artists would seek to sell their paintings in galleries where tourists were looking for works that depicted the landscapes of that area. She felt Jill would have more luck in such places than galleries in big cities. Jill thanked her for her suggestion. She immediately started researching cities and galleries that met those criteria.

Two weeks later, on September 16th, it appeared as though Jill's efforts tracking down Henry with art dealers might finally be paying off. She had made contact with Mountain Scapes, an upscale dealer in Ashville, North Carolina. She had inquired if they had any works by Henry Mack. The young lady who took Jill's call, without a moment's hesitation, promptly said they didn't. Jill then asked about Old Mill paintings or if they had ever sold any such works. At this point the young sales girl passed her off to the gallery's owner, Mr. Jenkins.

"Mister Jenkins, I am trying to locate any paintings by, or information about, an artist named Henry Mack. Your associate said you might be able to help me," Jill said.

"Off the top of my head, I can't say as how I recognize the name. Give me a moment and I will look at my new-fangled computer log to see if there is any record of my shop having sold any work by that artist…

"Yes, here it is, this goes way back to when I first opened my gallery twenty-five years ago. I can't believe I still have a record of this sale. Now I do remember a bit about this. It seems like I had a painting by this new artist who was painting in this area. I believe a well to do couple from somewhere in the northeast bought the work. Seems like a year or so later an art dealer from New York stopped by to see if I had any more such works. He came in to my shop maybe about once a year after that, for several years afterwards.

"If you like, I will see if I can find a card on the fellow. He may be able to provide you a bit more information. Oh, and one more thing, I believe this art dealer said the couple who bought the painting may have actually bought the property where the artist had painted," Mr. Jenkins told her.

"Thanks so much. By all means, I would love to talk to the New York art dealer. Do you by chance have the name of the couple who bought the painting?" Jill asked.

"Sorry, no. My records, for some reason, don't contain their name. Your best bet will be the art dealer in New York. I believe he had a fairly close connection with them," he commented.

Jill provided Mr. Jenkins her cell number. He promised to look for the dealer's card and call her within the next couple of days. Jill was ecstatic with the information she had obtained. She had to tell David at once. Sure enough, just as he had promised, Mr. Jenkins called Jill the following Monday with the information on the New York art dealer,

His name was Tim Elkins of Park Art Collections LLC. He had an address on Park Avenue and Mr. Jenkins gave her the phone number he found. Fortunately, both David and Jill's last class on Tuesday ended at 3 pm so they were to meet at David's apartment immediately after class and call Mr. Elkins. David and Jill realized that the contact information was nearly twenty years old and in all likelihood the gallery may have closed.

They were in luck. The call was answered with 'Park Art Collections'. When Jill asked for Mr. Elkins, his assistant told them Mr. Elkins was traveling to review a client's collection and would not be back in the office until Friday. On a whim, David asked if they could schedule an appointment with him in his office for that Friday or the next Monday. She indicated that his Friday afternoon schedule presently was open. She said that she would contact him and verify their appointment the first thing the next morning.

By the time Tim Elkins assistant called the next morning, David and Jill already had tentative reservations on a flight to New York on Friday morning. It was a lot of money to spend flying to New York for a weekend. Especially for something that might not pan out. Since neither had ever been to the Big Apple, at the very least it would be a nice mini vacation. Obviously neither sets of parents were too delighted with them taking off classes and spending hundreds of dollars for a weekend in New York.

Fortunately, their classes on Friday were not critical for either of them. Early Friday morning, David picked up Jill and they were off to the airport and the Big Apple. Not wanting to attempt driving in such a strange big city, they chose to take an Uber for the forty-five-minute drive to downtown. They soon were glad they chose not to drive amongst the canyons of miles and miles of buildings.

David and Jill had a quick lunch at a sidewalk café down the street from the gallery. Following a great lunch, eaten amongst a mass of people, they walked the two blocks down Park Avenue to their appointment at Park Art Gallery.

Mr. Elkins greeted the pair, "My assistant tells me you two young folks flew all the way from Atlanta up here to see me. I am intrigued about the purpose of your visit."

David led off by introducing himself and Jill to Mr. Elkins. David then said, "I will attempt to summarize our story. Jill, feel free to chime in.

"A painter named Henry Mack, was my great uncle. It seems he bequeathed two oil paintings of an Old Grist Mill before he died. My family got one and it turned out that Jill's family got the other. There was part of a curious note on the back of each painting. We are attempting to solve the mystery of the notes on the back of the paintings.

"We felt if we could learn more about the mysterious painter, Henry Mack, it might help. Apparently, a gallery in Ashville, North Carolina sold a mountain scene of Mack's about twenty-five years ago. The gallery owner, Mr. Jenkins, told us that he thought you knew the buyer of that painting and that those buyers were in turn, acquainted with Henry Mack.

"We were hoping you might put us in touch with that painting's owners so we may find out more about Henry Mack."

"I see. It just so happens; I do remember Mr. Jenkins and the clients you are speaking of. One facet of my business is cataloging and appraising art collections for wealthy clients. As you might understand, most of my cliental are very security conscience, private individuals. Confidentiality is one mainstay of my services; therefore, I can't divulge their name to you.

"What I can and will do is to contact this client and

explain your interest in the artist of their painting. I will see if they would be willing to meet with you. Not to get your hopes up, but this particular couple are now up in years and they are very friendly. I feel there is a fairly good chance they will agree to a meeting.

"I should hear back from them in the next week and will get in touch with you then. Since you have traveled all this way to see me, I must ask, have you two been to the Big Apple before?"

"No sir. This is our first trip," Jill replied.

"That being the case, you should take in a Broadway play while you are here. I happen to have a couple of tickets to the musical, '*Into the Woods*' for tomorrow night, if you would like them," he offered.

"Wow! That would be wonderful." They graciously accepted.

Leaving their meeting with Mr. Elkins, David commented to Jill, "I think that went well, what do you think?

"I agree, it went great! I believe we are on the right track to getting more information on your great uncle. Can you believe he even gave us tickets to a Broadway play? How marvelous of him."

David agreed. "So now for a bit of sightseeing? What do you say. Let's take the subway over to Central Park. I would like to see that, then maybe the Empire State building and the World Trade Building," David commented. They both agreed the sights in the Big Apple were very interesting, but there were just so many people. Too many.

It was a reasonably successful trip and one in which they both enjoyed their first Broadway play, though they had no idea how to dress for such an event. After a bit of worry, particularly on Jill's part, they just wore the nicest outfits they had brought. It turned out they were not too out of place. The play was great. Jill especially loved it, vowing that she wanted to return to see more plays. They agreed, next time they would be prepared to dress a bit nicer.

On the plane ride back Sunday afternoon, they discussed plans for their Thanksgiving and Christmas holidays. They held out hopes that they might get to meet the owners of the mountain painting in North Carolina before then.

Sure enough, a week after their New York adventure, David received a call from Mr. Elkins. He told David that he had spoken with the painting's owners, a Mr. and Mrs. Flanders, about setting up a meeting. They had agreed. Being curious himself, he planned to attend as well. Mr. Elkins had a couple of dates the couple had given him when they would be available. Both were in late October.

One date was October 26, a Saturday. That date worked best with David and Jill's school schedule. David promptly responded that the 26th date would be fine. He asked Mr. Elkins to thank the couple and to confirm a time and location where to meet in North Carolina.

That evening the painting's owner Mr. Flanders called David directly and invited both he and Jill to join he and his wife for lunch at their home near Lake Lure, North Carolina at 12:30 on the 26th. Mr. Flanders said that Mr. Elkins would also be joining them. David thanked Mr. Flanders profusely for extending the invitation.

"Guess what Jill? we have a lunch date with the Flanders in Lake Lure, North Carolina. We are to be there at 12:30 on the 26th. That shouldn't be too difficult, since according to the Waze App. Lake Lure is only a three plus hour drive. Great news, isn't it?" David boasted.

Finally, the 26th arrived. David picked Jill up at 8 am figuring that should allow plenty of time to get to Lake Lure. It was a beautiful Fall Day with the leaves in their full glory.

"Jilly, your blond hair matches the maples this morning. We have a chilly morning to go to the mountains. You cold? Need me to turn on a bit of heat?" David asked.

"No, I am fine. I do so love these cool mornings. I think Fall is becoming my favorite season. It's the time of year for a fire in the fireplace and you can open the windows a crack and sleep under a blanket," she added.

"Or sleep with a sweet warm special person snuggled next to you to keep you warm."

"I couldn't have put that better."

Three hours later as they approached Lake Lure, they listened closely to the directions being announced by the precise sounding voice of their GPS. The Flanders location looked to be about seven miles from Lake Lure. They left the main highway and began following a series of smaller roads, ending at the base of a mountain and a gated driveway. The drive appeared to lead upward to the summit of a small mountain or knoll. There was a call box and camera by the automatic gate. David promptly pushed the button and announced their presence.

His call at the gate was promptly answered. The person who answered the call said they were expected and the gate quickly swung open. They drove up what seemed like a mile long drive as it curved upward toward the summit. On top, they found a three-hundred-and-sixty-degree view of mountains, valleys, and even a distant view of the speck of water which they took to be Lake Lure.

The home, or rather estate, in which they parked in front of, was truly a large eloquent home. Despite its outward grandeur, the home's low profile blended in quite nicely with the mountain top. Jill nervously rang the doorbell that had a camera above it. Soon a doorman opened the door and welcomed them inside.

Almost immediately their hosts, the elderly Mr. and Mrs. Flanders appeared in the reception hall to greet the pair.

"Welcome to our home, you two young people. I am Fred Flanders and this is my wife, Sarah."

"Thanks so much for having us. I am David Mack and this is Jill Howard," David said, introducing them.

"Tim Elkins is due to join us, but as usually is the case with Mr. Elkins, he tends to be just a bit late for appointments. Anyway, please come on in to our study. I suppose we will wait a little while before lunching," Mr. Flanders said.

"David, am I to understand you are related to the painter Henry Mack?" Fred asked.

"Yes, Sir, he was my great uncle," David responded.

"Please no 'Sir' is necessary and also let's use first names if you don't mind. Now tell us your story and what you would like from us?"

"Jill, why don't you tell our hosts about our paintings and our quest," David requested.

"Sure, you see, David and I are college students. We were both taking an English course at the same time, but in separate classes. We had the same professor. We were each given an assignment to write a paper of something of interest. I chose to write about an Old Grist Mill painting my parents had, that I loved. Surprisingly, David here, wrote about an eccentric great uncle, Henry Mack. Our professor recognized that we had, in a sense and by chance, written about the same subject.

"Our professor introduced us. It became even more strange since we found out David's parents have another painting of the same old mill by Henry Mack. On the back of each painting there is part of a cryptic message. When these are combined, it read, *Find my match and it will be yours*," Jill said.

"So, you see, we are attempting to find out more about Uncle Henry and where this elusive Old Mill might be," David added.

"Wow, that is quite a story. This is some adventure you two have embarked on. I don't know how much help we can be, but we will tell you what we know about Henry Mack," Sarah said. "First let's have some lunch."

Over lunch, now with the tardy Tim Elkins having joined them, Fred explained how they had come to meet Henry Mack.

"It was twenty-five years ago and we had gone to Ashville to see the Biltmore house. While in Ashville we stopped into Mr. Jenkins gallery to browse. There we saw that striking landscape painting over there," he said, while pointing to a painting on the wall of the study. "We had already started collecting such paintings by that time. This painting was special. It was such an idyllic scene. You know a place of remote beauty.

"Mr. Jenkins said the artist was still painting in the North Carolina area and he put him in touch with us. The first question we asked him was where he had painted this idyllic painting. Yes, he brought us here. He even helped arrange for us to buy this property. Apparently, he had done such a thing for others who liked the locations where he painted. We owe it to your great uncle for this grand place where we are enjoying spending our golden years," Fred said.

"We stayed in touch with Henry for about three years after buying that painting. He even helped us in sighting our home here on this mountain top. The last time we got a note from him he was at a beach, painting what he claimed was the most beautiful beachy scene he ever saw. He didn't say where it was. So secretive you know.

"After that we lost track of him. I suspect that was due to his death. The last time we spoke to him, he said he had finally found his own special place, along with the love of his life. He never told us where it was or the name of his lady friend. I bet it just might be the Old Mill in your painting," Sarah added.

After a delicious lunch prepared by the couple's chef and a tour of their home and property, David and Jill thanked them. After saying their goodbyes, later that afternoon they headed back to Atlanta. They promised to stay in touch with the Flanders and let them know how their Old Mill search worked out.

"You know, David, even though they didn't know where the Old Mill was, they were great to talk to. They seemed to really like your uncle. The more I learn about him, the better I like him. Even if we never find the Old Mill, this has been a really great adventure, and you know what, you are not too bad for a boyfriend."

8. Finally, A *Nugget*

It had been two years and a great number of hours of research for the pair of lovebirds. One night in late April, after he had been reenergized by their recent trip to meet with the Flanders, David decided to run another Google search on H.M. Mack. The pair had performed a similar search on Google and other such sites at the start of their search, but to no avail. This time was to prove different. He got a hit.

What turned up was an old newspaper article entitled 'Eccentric H.M. Mack, and his Real Estate Business'. The article said this H.M. Mack was also a landscape artist. This must be his relative, David thought. He was overjoyed and wanted to share his find with Jill. But first he read the article.

This reporter has been on a hunt to discover the story behind a company called Great Lands Inc. and in particular the man behind this company, a Mr. H.M. Mack. We are interested in the mysterious land transactions of the company. What we have found, which granted is not a lot, is that Great Lands, Inc. appears to be a real estate investment company that acquires specific large parcels of pristine land. It appears as though Great

Lands then sells the parcels to wealthy individuals or land trusts for the preservation of the land. It also appears that these parcels are not being sold for development, as one might expect.

This all seems too good to be true, in this reporter's way of thinking. Efforts to gain more incite from the attorney who facilitated the transactions has thus far been unsuccessful as has been our efforts to interview the secretive, Mr. H.M. Mack. Hopefully we will be able to confirm what is really transpiring with these transactions in the near future.

The article appeared in a Denver Colorado newspaper in 1992, some thirty years earlier. David wondered if, by chance, this could this really be his great uncle. More work on this story was urgently needed. He must tell Jill at once. Though a bit late on a school night, he decided to call her with the news.

"Hah Jill, guess what, I think we may finally have a solid lead on Henry. I ran another Google search on him and got a hit. It was an old newspaper article. I think it is likely that the newspaper article has just recently been digitized and published on the web. It is from 1992. It seems we may have been looking for him in the wrong part of the country. We had talked about the mountains in the background of the paintings appeared larger than the Appalachians.

"I believe they are the Rockies. You see the article was from a Denver newspaper. Say, your family were from Colorado, weren't they?" David asked.

"Wow! That is great news. I can't believe Colorado. Yes, my relatives did come from there and I still have some there. What a coincidence. When do we leave?" She joked.

"Hold your horses. All we have is a possible new state

to look in. We don't have any new names other than the reporter who wrote an article thirty years ago, but I do feel like we may be getting a little closer to solving the mystery."

"I will be over after my last class tomorrow and we can plot how to find out more," she promised.

The pair had a pizza that David had picked up and a couple of beers he had stashed from his dad's supply. David had printed out the brief article he had found and after Jill perused it, she suggested they see what they could find out about the reporter who had written the piece. David announced he had already done so and came up empty.

"What if we contact the newspaper and see if there is anyone there that knows the reporter or for that matter about this company, *Great Lands, Inc.*?" Jill suggested.

"Good idea but it may be too late today to get much information, let's see ... it would be two hours earlier there, so five o'clock, probably be better to call tomorrow, don't you think."

"Yah, you are probably right. Perhaps our lunch time might be about right there. Will you make the call or would you like me to?" she asked.

"Oh, I will do it. I am out of class early tomorrow. We shouldn't hold our breaths though, seeing as how that has been thirty years. He has probably left the paper or for that matter he may be dead. As for the company, since Uncle Henry has been gone twenty years, I suspect his company is likely gone as well. Despite all that, you never know what we might turn up. We are very persistent detectives, don't you think?"

Since they both had final exams the next day, they cut

the evening short to study. About an hour after Jill left, David's cell rang. It was Jill.

"Well David, unfortunately I found the answer to the first question on the internet. I found an old obituary for that reporter. Apparently, he died in an accident soon after the article appeared. Guess that is why there was never any follow-up article," Jill reported.

"At least it said he died in an accident and not murdered. If it had said murdered, I would have wondered. Thanks for that piece of info. Keep your fingers crossed that I will have better luck tomorrow with Great Lands, Inc. Say, though, aren't you supposed to be studying?" David asked.

"What, you are now acting like my parents, give me a break!" she shot back.

"Guess since you are smarter than lover boy here, you don't need to study." David closed with, "Want to take my exam tomorrow, dear?"

Just as he had promised, David made contact with the Denver Post Newspaper the next day in an attempt to find out more about *Great Lands*. He had no luck. The only advice he got was to check their archives on the internet. The person he spoke with suggested that he might check with the Colorado Secretary of State's office, to see if the company was still in business.

A week later, exams were over. Time to get ready for summer jobs and to have time to spend on the mill search. The next step they felt was to do more research on Henry's business. Hopefully they could find out what had become of it and perhaps if there had been an old mill amongst his properties.

Luck was finally on David and Jill's side. When, after some time, David got in touch with a clerk in the Secretary of State's office, she verified that the company appeared no longer registered. What she did graciously offer to do, was to research when the registration expired and see who was the last legal representative for *Great Lands, Inc.*

The next day the clerk, Judy, called David back and reported that the last year of incorporation was the year 2001. She said, at that time, the legal representative was Mr. Bill Brooks of the law firm Brooks and Partners, LLP. David thanked her profusely. After he hung up, he calculated based on the date Henry died that it would have been about right for Henry's company to be closed the year after Henry's death. David immediately looked up the phone number for the law firm in Denver.

When David reported the information to Jill, she wanted to come over the next day at 5 o'clock which would be 3 o'clock Denver time. They would be on the call together when they called Mr. Bill Brooks. They had expected to be put on a long hold or be told that Mr. Brooks was not in the office. Mr. Brooks assistant asked what she could tell him was the nature of their call. They told her, "Mr. Henry Mack and his Old Mill paintings."

Almost at once, she came back on the line and said, "Mr. Brooks will be happy to speak to you now. I will put you right through."

The pair were astonished at the rapid response.

David explained that he and Jill each had one of Henry Mack's paintings of an old mill which may be located in Colorado. David said that they had located him from an old newspaper article and wondered if they could ask him what he knew about Henry Mack. The pair went on to explain that David was a relative of Henry Mack.

There was an uncomfortable brief moment of silence. Finally, Bill Brooks said that he would be very excited to meet with both of them at his office in Colorado. He said that he could provide them with a great deal of information about Henry and his Old Mill. He closed by encouraging them to come and see him at their earliest convenience.

"Hallelujah! It looks like we may have finally found someone who has the answers to the paintings," Jill gushed. The two were jumping, and hugging in the excitement of the moment.

"Yep, does appear so," David said, then adding, "When do we go?"

"Immediately!" Jill shot back.

9. The Attorney & A Tale

Their plane landed in Denver right on schedule. Since Jill had family in Colorado, she had been to Denver before. David had never been there. He was quite excited to see the snowcapped Rockies. Jill gave him her window seat as they started their descent into Denver. They both marveled at the huge modern airport. Quickly they picked up their rental car. He entered the attorney's address in his phone GPS and they were off to the big city of Denver.

David marveled at the snow-covered peaks to the west. "I really want to drive into the mountains while we are here," he exclaimed.

"So, we shall," Jill commented, "but first I am beside myself to find out the answers to all our questions about Henry and his Old Mill."

"When was the last time you were in Colorado? Does anything look familiar?" David asked.

"Oh, I have been out here quite a few times. The last time was maybe two years ago," she responded. "My uncle and his family live up near Golden, and my aunt's family are down at Colorado Springs."

"Have you been skiing out here?"

"Sure have, at Beaver Creek. This is real skiing out here. Back at Gatlinburg, skiing is more beginners' slopes," she said in a gloating manner.

When they arrived at the address they had been given over the phone, they found it to be an imposing modern high-rise office tower in the heart of downtown Denver. Fortunately, there was a convenient parking garage next to the office tower.

"Pretty nice digs," David commented as they entered the lobby. Jill agreed.

Moving to the building directory they confirmed that the law offices of Brooks and Partners, LLP was listed at suite 1700, the same suite as they had been given by Mr. Brooks Assistant.

"My but this must be a rather large firm. It looks like they have a whole floor," David said.

When the elevator door opened on the seventeenth floor, they were greeted by an elaborate lobby with two receptionists sitting at a booth in the center along a wall.

"Ma'am, I am David Mack and we have an 11 o'clock appointment with Mr. Brooks, Jr." David announced.

"Yes sir, I believe he is expecting you. It will be just a moment," she said. "Please have a seat and I will tell him you have arrived."

Within a very few minutes they were escorted into a grand corner office.

"So, you are the couple I spoke to over the phone about Henry Mack," Mr. Brooks said as he introduced himself as Bill Brooks Jr. He asked them to call him Bill. "So, tell me again how you managed to find me and just how you might be connected to Mr. Mack?"

Jill related the story of the two essays and the Old Mill painting as well as all the research they had done that led to him.

Finally, Mr. Brooks asked, "Did you mention a second old mill painting?"

"Yes, that's right Jill has one and I have the other. There is part of a strange note on the back of both."

"And Jill, just how did you come by your painting?" Mr. Brooks asked.

"I believe it came from my family, maybe from a great aunt," Jill responded.

"Your great aunt…Her name wouldn't possibly have been Carolyn, would it?" he asked.

"Why yes, I believe so."

At that comment, he paused a moment, then to their amazement, Mr. Brooks started to cry. He excused himself, saying he would be right back.

"Was he crying?" Jill asked David once Bill left the room.

"I think so," David responded quietly.

The pair set there uncomfortably for a few minutes waiting on the attorney to return.

"I am so sorry about that; you see this is a pretty emotional thing for me. David, your great uncle, Henry Mack, was a dear friend who I knew quite well.

"As an attorney, I should require you to show me the paintings before I tell you this story but I am going to trust what you have told me is true. I will share a story I have kept for years. Actually, the story starts with my father, Mr. Brooks Sr., who founded this firm.

"As my father told me about forty years ago, a middle-aged man, about the same age as my father back then, came to see him to enlist his help with some real estate transactions. From that first meeting, he stressed secrecy in all his dealings. I have attempted to maintain that requirement as I took over your great uncle's dealings. The fact that it took you two years to find me, attests to my successful efforts in that regard.

"You mentioned a newspaper article. I well remember that reporter. He was persistent. Fortunate for me, but sad for him, he was killed in an automobile accident shortly after that article appeared. Again, it was Henry's desire that everything he did be kept confidential. I can assure you Henry didn't have him 'knocked off' if that is what you are thinking.

"Back to my father's and my first dealings with him that I was aware of. Henry had a great love for the beauty of nature. That beautiful painting on that wall over there is one of his that he gave to my father. Henry's passion was preserving beautiful pieces of land. He would find these beautiful parcels on his hiking and painting travels. If the spots were private lands, then he would arrange to option or buy them. He would then find wealthy people who shared his sense for preservation to buy the properties to save them from development.

"Henry made a fair amount of money with these transactions, but it was never about the money. I believe a great number of his land purchasing clients were also those he had sold paintings to. As you may have noticed, there aren't too many of his paintings in galleries or museums.

"Everything seemed to be going along fine for Henry. He was a sixty-year-old man who had never been married. Henry enjoyed his painting which led him to travel to interesting places. Then Carolyn came along. As I recall, he met her at one of his exhibits in Denver.

"She was a widow. Henry was single, never married. She was quite lovely. I believed she came from an old Colorado family. The two instantly fell deeply in love and were seldom apart. After three months, Henry proposed to Carolyn. She accepted and they were to be married. I believe their wedding was to be in the spring of 1999. It is hard for me to believe she was your great aunt, Jill.

"Also, like Henry, she loved nature and so enjoyed his paintings. About this same time, Henry discovered a property with an old mill on part of the property. Instantly he knew it was to be the place he and Carolyn were to live. This place was to be a surprise for her. He set about planning and starting construction on a large two-story log home for the pair there on the old mill property. Henry even envisioned them being married there.

"Soon after he discovered the property, he set about doing a painting of the Old Mill. He had kept the mill property a secret from her. His plan was to surprise her with a painting of it.

"In February, as he was planning to unveil his surprise for her, tragically, she slipped on some ice while crossing a street. She hit her head and died in a hospital a day later. Henry was devastated. It took the life right out of him.

Though he went on to complete his log home later that year, he never moved into what was to have been his and Carolyn's Old Mill home.

"What Henry did do was to restore the old mill and to upgrade access into the property. It was at that point he formulated this idea of preserving the property for some other young couple to enjoy, as he had been prevented from doing with Carolyn.

"As part of his plan, he did another painting of the mill. He gave his first, the larger one, to Carolyn's family in hopes two young lovers such as you two would discover the paintings. Just as it amazingly seems to have happened."

Again Mr. Brooks appeared to start weeping as he continued.

The emotional story had brought Jill and David to the point of tears as well.

"At the time, my dad and I both felt, though this was a very romantic thing, it was also very unlikely for such a thing to occur. But here you two are!

"Once Henry had fixed up the mill and put this scheme in place, his health declined very rapidly. He passed away from cancer only about eighteen months after Carolyn's death.

"Since he was not close with other family members, he left it to me to prepare his will and take care of his final arrangements. He insisted that I get his second mill painting to his closest living relative. David, that being your dad, I suppose.

"Even in this he demanded secrecy. I never told your dad the story about the two paintings when I sent the painting to him. Please tell me just how did you two meet and and came to bring the two paintings together.

"David, why don't you tell the story. I am a bit too emotional right now," a teary-eyed Jill said.

"Sure, I am as well a bit emotional at all this. You see, Bill, as unbelievable as it appears, and certainly this whole thing is just so remarkable, we met at college. We both had English classes. We were in different classes, but had the same professor. This professor gave us an assignment to write a paper on a subject requiring research. It just so happened that Jill chose to write about a favorite family painting, the Old Mill.

"I, on the other hand, chose an eccentric great uncle, Henry Mack. Our professor introduced us, realizing that we had, coincidentally chosen the same subject. After we met, a comparison of the two paintings revealed the strange notes. After two years chasing the Old Mill, here we are."

"This is like some whopper of a tale. It is almost too strange to be true. Having known the dreamer Henry was, it must be true. I would say you two owe your professor a big thank you. It appears he has set you about something that has brought you two to find love for each other. In addition to that, perhaps a sizable worth of property and other material things as well," Bill said.

"Per Henry's instructions, I am to verify the two paintings and the inscriptions on the back of them. Only then can we read his Will."

"When do you think you can bring me your paintings to verify?" Bill asked.

"Hopefully in a couple of weeks," David volunteered.

"That will be great. Then we can conclude this matter," Bill said. "In the meantime, you two wouldn't possibly like to see the Old Mill of your search, would you?" He jokingly asked them.

"You bet we would!" Jill piped up.

David responding, "Of course … ASAP!"

10. A Visit To The Old Mill

It was a Wednesday, the fourth of June 2021. David and Jill were excited beyond their wildest dreams to think that after two long years they were finally to see the Old Mill they had been chasing. Even more than that, it appeared the Old Mill might actually soon be theirs.

Bill Brooks had given them the address and directions how to get to the mill site. He said the gate into the property would be locked and that he would meet them at the gate. David had entered the location into the GPS application on his phone. He felt he could get there without too much trouble. Bill had told them it was about an hour and a half drive from Denver. Driving into the mountains was an exciting shared experience for the pair, especially for David, who had never been to the Rockies.

According to Bill, the property was located in the front range of the Rockies, down to the southwest toward Aspen, though not quite that far. He had described the location as a truly beautiful spot with a beautiful tumbling mountain stream. According to Bill, the associated property with the mill totaled one hundred acres. It backed up to National Forrest land.

The pair had traveled west on Interstate 70 and were to get off at the Silverthorne exit and take highway 91 toward Leadville. The road leading to the mill property turned off of Highway 91 shortly before Leadville. It sounded very simple. David began to wonder if it would be?

It was 10 am when they reached the first turnoff for Silverthorne. They had plenty of time since they were not to meet Bill until 11:30. They were to meet him at the gate to the driveway into the mill. Bill was bringing the key to the gate. Bill also had volunteered to provide the three of them with picnic lunches to eat at the mill.

Locating Mill Creek Road off highway 91 was a bit of a challenge. The GPS had a vague map of the area, and spotty cell phone reception, requiring more searching for road signs than they were used to. Upon realizing they were almost to Leadville, they decided it wise to stop and ask directions. They backtracked to what seemed to be an out of place McDonalds, a couple of miles back. This worked out nicely as they both needed a bathroom break. They had no idea if there would be facilities at the mill.

The restaurant employees seemed clueless about the location of Mill Creek Road. Quite fortunately, there was an elderly woman in line who overheard them ask directions. She spoke up telling them how far back the road it was to the Mill Creek turn-off and giving them an identifying landmark. She told them to look for a single pine just off the highway. She said it was referred to as the 'Lonesome Pine'. Jill thanked the woman for her help.

Finally, they found Mill Creek Road. They proceeded down the paved, barely two-lane road for about a mile. They noticed only a couple of driveways off the road. Soon they came to a rather large frame house and past that driveway they saw a sign that read 'Road End / Private Property.' Just past the sign there was a double metal gate across the road.

Despite the minor problem with finding Mill Creek Road, they arrived a bit early at 11:15. They had only been parked there about five minutes when Bill showed up.

"Have any problem getting here?" he asked as he took out a ring of keys.

"No, not much, only had to stop for directions once. This Mill Creek Road is a bit hard to spot," David commented.

"Yes, I guess it could be. Having been here so many times over the years, I forgot how it might be difficult for strangers to this area. Sorry for your difficulty."

With the gate unlocked and opened, Bill invited them to get into his vehicle so he could take them in to the property. The driveway was shrouded with large evergreen trees. It seemed they were entering a dense forest. What a grand entrance they commented. A short distance down the drive they came to a curve, then right beyond that was a modern steel and concrete bridge spanning an extremely active and rather wide stream.

"This, as you might gather is Mill Creek. It runs through Henry's property and is what powered the old mill," Bill said.

After another curve in the driveway, a cleared area appeared. There they saw a rather large rustic log structure. From the appearance of the logs, it was evident this structure was of a somewhat recent vintage. It also appeared quite different from the structure in the Old Mill painting. This certainly did not seem to be the mill building from the painting.

Bill quickly explained, "This is what Henry called the 'main house'." He said Henry had started it as a home for he and Carolyn to live in, prior to her sudden death. Henry went on and finished it, but as far as he knew, Henry never lived in it. He said it was, "for his 'love'."

As they parked in front of the two-story house, it appeared to be a cross between a mountain ski house and a cottage. Bill explained that Henry had designed it himself. The structure before them was a rather massive log affair of two stories with a slightly faded dark green metal roof. The logs looked to have been freshly stained within the last few years. Only a scattering of pine needles and leaves cluttered the full length covered front porch.

From the outside, the house was quite charming. It was closely flanked by pines and larches and massive boulders.

Jill said, "I can't help but ask, where is the Old Mill from the painting?"

"Be patient, young lady, you will see it soon enough." With that Bill once again pulled out his ring of keys and invited them inside the house. They stepped up onto the porch and he soon had the door open.

The house was rather dark, a bit musty, and devoid of furnishings. Bill turned on the lights and started leading them thru toward the back side of the house. They had entered what appeared to be a great room. Suddenly they saw it. There, through a large window, appeared the Old

Mill that they had searched for so long. The view seemed almost identical to the paintings. It was quite an emotional moment for all three.

From the great room there were glass doors opening out to a deck. They walked out on the deck which wrapped around two sides of the house. One corner of the deck was enclosed as a screened in porch. In addition to the dramatic view of the Old Mill, they saw the mountains which now seemed close at hand and formed a perfect backdrop for the old mill.

The deck on the left side of the house protruded almost to the edge of the roaring stream. Though the exterior of the building and the decks were a bit weathered, after twenty odd years, it was evident the house had been well maintained.

Back inside, the great room had a fairly large stone fireplace. Continuing their tour, Bill led them into the opposite end of the main floor where they found an almost modern kitchen of year 2000 vintage. Beyond the kitchen, Bill opened a door to a grand master bedroom containing another smaller stone fireplace. Doors from the bedroom led to a bath and then there was another glass door which led out onto the deck.

Proceeding up the staircase off the entry, they discovered three more bedrooms, each with a grand view as well. Then there was a large modern bath.

Though the house was largely unfurnished, there was a round wooden table and four chairs on the covered porch area at the rear with a grand view of the mill. Bill suggested that they take their lunch there. He asked David to get the cooler from his SUV while he carried in a lunch hamper. Despite it being slightly chilly, it was a delightful setting to dine.

"This place is just so, so amazing. I love it!" Jill exclaimed.

"What a wonderful place Uncle Henry found," David said. "Do you know how he came to discover this place?"

"Well, David, let me tell you a bit more about your uncle. As a painter of nature and scenery, he traveled a good bit in his younger years. He was always seeking out locations to paint that had not been spoiled by man. Along the way, he discovered a number of what he called his special places. He also met a number of wealthy folks to whom he had sold paintings. Some of them were so taken with the locations he painted; they asked if he would see if those properties might be available to be acquired. That is how he started Great Lands, Inc.

"My father incorporated the company for Henry thirty years ago. I believe Henry asked a finder's fee of about ten percent to locate and facilitate the purchase of pristine properties for clients. I also believe he was even more successful in that endeavor than as an artist.

"He tried to keep his 'Great Lands' work somewhat private for the sake of his wealthy clients' privacy. He wasn't really interested in becoming a real estate agent. That newspaper article you mentioned was one attempt to expose his work. Fortunately, or unfortunately the reporter died before he could dig deeper in to 'Great Lands'.

"Henry told me that he was looking for an old mill to paint. Someone told him about this mill. So, this mill property was one such find that Henry stumbled across. Henry was immediately captivated with the property and bought it. He told me that he couldn't sell it, therefore he never did any paintings of it, that is, besides the two that you two have. Guess that makes your paintings rather special, don't you think?"

"Absolutely!" David responded.

"Bill, when did you first see this place?" Jill asked.

"Henry knew this property was special the first time he saw it some twenty-eight years ago. He was very excited, insisting my dad and I come out right after he closed on the deal. We both told him we felt he had a great find here. Over the years before his death, he had my dad and I out here on numerous occasions. Looking back on it though, none were quite as special as the first time. Henry was just so excited about the place.

"Back then, he had such grand plans. It was here he planned to spend his golden years with his Carolyn."

"So, let me tell you a bit more about the property and then we can walk around, if you wish. The entire property consists of one hundred acres. On the property there are four buildings. This is the main house. Off to the right, nestled in the woods, is a 'caretakers' cottage. Next to that is a combination storage shed and garage building. Then, of course, there is the main attraction, the Old Mill.

"Actually, as you can see, there is another old building across Mill Creek from the Mill. I don't recall if Henry ever found out what it was used for. It was inconvenient with its location across the stream. To my knowledge, Henry never used it for anything except perhaps some storage. Henry said it was just part of the pastoral scenery, therefore he could not bring himself to tear it down.

"Let me tell you what I know about the mill. The mill, though it appears to be a more common grist mill, was in fact used to produce power. I would expect it would be easy to use it to grind grain, as well as to produce power. Power was a real luxury in the early years before public power was available. I believe the mill produced power for the mining operation on this site."

"Can it still produce electricity? Could the houses be 'off the grid' so to speak?" David asked, quite excitedly.

"That's a good question. At the time of Henrys death, he had it producing some power. About the same time that the houses on Mill Creek Road were built, public utility electric lines were brought into this area. We had the buildings on the property connected to public power then. I would guess with some effort, this whole compound could be powered off the mill if one chose to do so," Bill responded.

"Before we make our tour, there is one other aspect of the property that I should tell you about. It has an old mine on it. That is right, the property even comes with a gold mine. Back in the 1890s, a shaft was sunk at the base of the mountain off to our right. I believe they were mining for gold. I doubt much was found or the mineworks would have been more extensive," Bill commented.

"Unbelievable, all this and a gold mine as well! This is just too much," Jill spouted.

"How on earth could Uncle Henry have afforded this place?" David asked.

"This property was expensive back then. It would be a

lot more so today. David, as I said earlier, Henry made a lot off his property sales business and the sale of his paintings. He led a modest lifestyle. Over time he became quite wealthy," Bill explained.

They started their tour behind the house where an old stone walkway led to the Old Mill. The mill had an overshot waterwheel. The rushing streams water flowed through a chute and cascaded onto the top of the waterwheel turning a main shaft which was geared to a power generator. The mill wheel was in an idle status and not turning the generator. David could see hours of fun tinkering with this fascinating big toy.

As they stood there looking at the old mill, David pulled up a picture he had taken of his painting. He began comparing his painting picture with the structure before him. Clearly it was the same old mill, yet it appeared somewhat different.

One change he noticed immediately was the newer looking wood shakes covering all parts of the roof. It also appeared the planking on the walls may have been repaired and boards replaced. These changes were likely to have been done in the interest of preservation, he surmised. Neither detracted from the rustic appearance.

David was very anxious to venture inside the mill. Bill was pushing the pair and said he only had time for a quick peak. David, on the other hand, was very curious with the workings of the mill.

"Come on, Jill, let's explore the inside," David begged.

"It is probably dirty with cobwebs, spiders, and rodents in there."

"Maybe not, I will go in first and turn on the lights," he said while Bill found the right key and opened the squeaky old door. David finally found the switch and two faint bulbs produced an eerie glow producing shadows of old equipment and various large items. With Bill's urging him they had to leave soon, David was unable to have much time to figure out the mill operation. I will be back here again soon, he thought.

Next, they made their way down a path to the 'caretakers' quarters. Bill explained that Tim Hargrove, the caretaker who had been there ever since Henry's death, had been forced to move to Leadville the past year due to his wife's health. Tim still came by to check on the place twice a month.

Bill went on to explain that the 'caretakers' cabin was the first new building Henry built on the property. Originally, he built it to have a place to stay while he built the main house for him and Carolyn. She had died halfway through the construction of the new house he was building. After her death, Henry finished the new Mill House, though he chose to never move into it. Instead, Henry lived in the cabin for a little over a year before his death.

Once Henry died, Bill said it was apparent that the property would need a caretaker. This was provided for in the terms of Henry's peculiar will. Tim was a natural since he was familiar with the property, having helped build the new mill house. Bill commented again that David should meet him.

Looking inside the cabin, they noticed it had two bedrooms, a small kitchen, a single bath, and a main room/ den with a nice stone fireplace. They noticed a neatly stacked wood pile near the cabin. It was quaint and it also looked to have been well maintained.

From there they went to the shed. Inside they discovered an assortment of tools and building materials. The shed building also had an open metal shed roof on the side. Bill said that was where Henry, and later Tim, kept their vehicles.

"Now I expect you want to see the 'gold mine' don't you?" Bill asked.

"Of course, we do. I have never seen one before," Jill piped up.

"Well, we will have to be quick since I am due back to my office for a meeting at 4:30. You will now see why I suggested you wear hiking boots as I am doing," he commented.

With that he led them about one hundred yards up an overgrown path. The path led toward the mountain that towered over them to their North. The trail became steeper as it weaved through the forest. Suddenly they came out in a clearing populated with scrub trees growing on the old mine tailings. There before them and about seventy-five feet above them was a locked, gated mineshaft. The shaft was marked with a weathered sign saying *Danger—Do Not Enter.*

"OK you two, I must run. You can hang around a while if you like. Just do be careful and please stay out of the mine. Kindly lock up and close the gate and lock it when you leave. You can drop the keys back by my office tomorrow. Let me know when you can return with your paintings so I can prepare documents. Assuming the paintings are as you say, this all may soon be yours.

"Congratulations, you two kids! I am sure David; your uncle Henry would be thrilled for you two. I am pretty happy for you as well. I never guessed when Henry sprung this craziness on me that such a thing could possibly happen," Bill said as he departed.

"So, Jill what do you think of what is soon to be our little piece of the world?"

"It is fantastic. This has to be a dream. It appears you are going to have a special place in Colorado."

"No. <u>We</u> are going to have this special place. Henry left it to the owners of both paintings. To the pair who solved the mystery. That be, you and I. We are in this together. Whatever we get, we share," David said.

Jill suggested, "Let's go down to the mill, take off our shoes, and dangle our feet in the water, like the boy in the painting."

"Are you kidding? That water is snow melt from the mountains. It has to be freezing. Bet I can keep my feet in longer," he challenged her.

"We will have to see about that," Jill responded.

Sitting there, side by side with their feet freezing, David managed to say while shivering, "You know if you don't mind, I believe a kiss might warm me up." She laughed as she leaned over to kiss him.

"Yep, that did help," David chirped up. Once their feet thawed a bit, the pair realized it was getting late and they had an hour and a half drive back to their hotel in Denver. Reluctantly, they locked up and walked back out to their car parked at the gate. Both vowed to come back in a couple of weeks to finalize ownership of their Old Mill.

On the flight back home, they discussed issues they had yet to face. One huge issue was how to explain their new found fortune. Another was what it might mean for their careers. They had shared with their families their search over the past two years. They had yet to tell anyone they had solved Henry's puzzle. Likewise, they had not mentioned about their meeting with the attorney and the very big prize they had apparently won.

"You know why don't we hold off mentioning the meeting with Bill Brooks, and that we are getting the Mill Property. Let's wait until we have signed the paperwork in a couple of weeks. What do you think?" David asked.

"Do you think we can keep the secret that long?"

"I know it will be tough, but let's try."

11. Claiming The Prize

It was a real challenge to come up with a good explanation
for parents and employers as to why David and Jill wanted
to make another trip to Colorado two weeks after they just
got back. One thought they discussed was just telling family the truth and even inviting some of them to join them.
David had a special reason for not doing that. All they told
anyone was they had found a source that was going to take
them to see the mill they had been seeking for so long.

David was especially nervous about the trip. Everything
had to be just perfect. He realized that he would have to
ask Bill Brooks for his assistance with one item. He felt
he must have champagne for the occasion and still being
slightly too young to buy it, he must ask Bill. A few days
before their flight, he placed a call to Bill to confirm their
appointment. He explained to Bill that he was planning
to propose to Jill the weekend they were in Colorado and
asked if he could obtain a bottle of bubbly for him to have.
He asked Bill to not mention it to Jill as he wished to
surprise her on Saturday. Bill said he would be more than
happy to pick out a special bottle.

A few days before they were to fly out, Jill brought her

painting over to David's apartment. David had visited an art store and obtained a wooden packing crate of sufficient size for both paintings. With a great deal of padding, they carefully packed the paintings. After adding numerous FRAGILE labels, they were ready to take them to the airport to be checked as baggage on their flight.

Their flight arrived in Denver at 10 am mountain time. They were to meet Bill at his office at 11:30. He had invited them to have lunch with him. So far so good. The crate containing the paintings appeared to be undamaged at baggage claim, much to their relief. After grabbing a rental SUV, they were on their way downtown.

Bill Brooks greeted them, "Glad to see my young "Mill Owners" again. What have we here?" he asked as each of them proudly showed him the paintings they carried. "Looks like the two paintings Henry described. And yes, they have, what appears to be, his handwritten notes on the back. I still can't believe how this crazy scheme of Henry's turned out."

"You two ready to be mill owners?" Bill asked.

"Yes sir!" They both exclaimed, "We sure are!"

"Well, let's grab some lunch and when we get back, we can sign the papers I have prepared. After that, I will be able to finally close out Henry's estate. There is a nice restaurant just down the street. It will be a chance to stretch our legs a bit. What do you think of our cool refreshing mountain air?"

"It is wonderful. Sure, beats the heat and humidity back East," Jill responded.

Over lunch Bill told them a bit more about Henry. He

also mentioned his good fortune having had Tim Hargrove to look after the place all the years since Henry's death. Based on the last time he had thoroughly inspected the property he felt everything there should be in good order.

Back at his office, Bill laid out a series of papers for all three to sign. He had other members of his staff come in to notarize and witness the signatures. Bill explained to them,

"There will of course, be some taxes for you to pay on the inheritance. However, the way Henry and I structured this, the taxes should be minimal. You see, when Henry sold the property to his trust, he did so at an inflated price, thereby limiting the appreciated value for you to be taxed on. Also, as you will soon see, his will is leaving you, as his heirs, with an abundance of funds to pay for quite a lot.

"Now for the balance of Henry's estate. Since the Will provides that the owners of the paintings shall, in addition to the mill property, also inherit the balance of Henry's estate, you are entitled to that as well.

THE WILL

Bill said, "Now that I am satisfied that you two are, in fact, the legal heirs to Henry Mack's estate and comply with the terms set out in his Will, of which I serve as executor, I will now read Henry's Will."

My good friend, Bill Brooks, knows quite well that I am a bit peculiar, therefore when it came to writing my 'Will", I told him I wanted to write it my way. He agreed. To start this, I am going to tell you what he may have already attempted to.

Having no close relatives, I had to decide what to do with those few things I had. You know, things that meant a lot to me. Had my dear Carolyn lived, most of this would have been hers. Sadly, it was not to be. When I proposed the quest involving the two paintings, I can assure you, Bill told me this was a completely ridiculous idea. Fortunately, I was able to convince him to go along and help me implement it.

The fact you are here today and reading this means you must meet the criteria that I set out for my dear friend, administrator, and executor, Bill Brooks.

Part 1. Stipulations / Assets

Item 1. Henry Morgan Mack has established trust funds which contains the balance of his investments including stocks, bonds, cash, and other tangible assets. This trust is to be bequeathed to party or parties as designated below in Part II.

Item 2. Henry Morgan Mack has established a trust fund with assets sufficient to pay the taxes, utilities, maintenance, etc. on a parcel of land and the structure thereon, 'heretofore referred to as the Old Mill Place'. Said trust is to pay all associated cost until April 30, 2025. At that time if the designated beneficiaries as outlined have not been established as per Part II, then the property is to be sold and all proceeds are to be distributed to the beneficiary or beneficiaries as defined in Part II

Item 3. Paintings—All unsold works in my possession at the time of my death are to go to the Denver Metropolitan Museum of Art to be dealt with as they see fit.

Item 4. Personal Effects—All are to be disposed of by my Executor as he sees fit.

Part 2. Beneficiaries

It is my desire that my two paintings of my Old Mill be used to determine my Beneficiaries. Perhaps one will be an heir, as one of the paintings is being given to a family member. My desire is that whoever connects the two paintings with my Old Mill and then seeks out Mr. Bill Brooks, they shall inherit the Old Mill Property. Should one of these two be a direct heir of mine, that individual shall inherit the trust funds containing all my other assets.

In the event no two people in possession of the two mill paintings have come forward by April 30, 2025, then Mr. Bill Brooks is directed to sell the Old Mill property and the proceeds from that as well as my main trust funds are to be split evenly 50% to my nearest heir under the age of 30 and 50% is to go to charities as my Executor may select. My fondest hope would be for a young relative of mine and likewise of Carolyn will be the ones who come up with the prize.

Bill announced, "There was a bit more legalese in the balance of the Will, in order to comply with state law, but that sums it up in a nutshell. I must say, when your great uncle proposed this manner for the disposal of his assets, I was dismayed. I never thought two individuals, especially two young people such as you and Jill, who are related to both Henry and Carolyn would solve the challenge and come forward before the deadline.

"You did. I am so glad. I am sure that if Henry was here today, he would be delighted.

"Per Henry's instructions the estate was to be invested in an annuity. Since the annuity has matured, based on time held, the funds could be taken as one lump sum or paid out over a period of ten years.

"From the numbers I recently ran, you would receive a lump sum now of approximately one million four hundred thousand or one hundred-seventy-five thousand a year for the next ten years. You may want to talk this over and let me know so I can get checks prepared," Bill announced.

"I must point out one peculiar item in the Will. It is something, I apologize, for not having an answer concerning. Shortly before Henry passed away, he asked me to change 'trust fund' to plural 'trust funds'. I am only aware of the one trust fund mentioned above. Unfortunately, Henry never explained the reason for his making this change, despite my prying. I guess what I am saying, there may be other funds out there which we may never know of."

"Wow!" David shouted. "Do you mean we get all that in addition to the Mill?"

"I am speechless," Jill said.

"You are two very lucky young detectives. Again, you probably owe your professor something special for facilitating your meeting. As to the mill property, you will each need to sign affidavit's releasing each other's half interest in this estate. On a similar note, that is why I had both of you bring me notarized affidavits from your parents establishing your total ownership of the paintings. Henry would not have wanted any disputes. Certainly, I don't either," Bill said.

With the signing of the papers, Bill stated the deed would be recorded and copies sent to them within thirty days. He reminded them to instruct him how to pay out the balance of the annuity so he could send them checks.

"Good luck you two, I wish you all the best. Please keep in touch. If there is anything I can ever do for you, please call me. Here are all of the keys to the Mill buildings and gate. I have also given you the caretakers' contact information and I believe you will find him willing to help in anything you need.

"Here are a couple of housewarming gifts for you two. One is for David, the smaller one and here Jill this larger one is for you. I would request you wait to open them until tomorrow when you are rested and at your new home. Hope you enjoy," Bill said.

David and Jill, both thanked him for his gifts and everything he had done for them and for, David's uncle, Henry Mack.

"Say, David and Jill, if you don't mind my asking, when are you two getting married? David, you have proposed, haven't you?"

That question prompted a coughing fit from David. *Surely, he isn't going to give away my surprise he thought.*

Jill responded, "Well, now that we have found our Mill perhaps, David here, can think of something other than the Old Mill."

The question of marriage left the pair blushing and trying to change the subject as they bid good bye to Bill. *David all the time thinking, Bill how could you?*

Since they had their two paintings to carry as well as the gifts and papers, Bill offered to help carry their things to their vehicle.

David and Jill were beside themselves as they headed out on the drive to what was now truly their Old Mill.

Jill spoke first, "David, tell me this is not just a dream. This can't really have happened, can it?"

"I agree, it does seem like a dream. To think, this is what those hand written notes on the back of two old paintings meant. Quite remarkable. Can you imagine what our parents will say?" David asked.

"They will certainly be as shocked. They will just flip out," she said.

"You are sure right about that!"

"What do you say, we check out of our hotel then head back to our new home for a quick visit before it gets dark. Maybe we could find a hotel in Leadville for tonight. That would be a lot closer," David said.

"That will be great. We can check out the town a bit. Sounds like a grand plan for a fun day. We must get furniture so we can stay in the house soon."

David thought to himself, becoming a bit nervous, only if you knew, Jill, what a day we have in store for tomorrow. On the drive back to Henry's Mill, which they were getting used to calling DJ's Mill, they discussed what they might need to do about the property. They definitely wanted to keep it. They both agreed they had no desire to sell it. They also agreed they probably needed to meet Tim the caretaker, who Bill had been using. They would likely need to enlist his services.

David suggested that they go to Leadville first to find a hotel for the night before the short drive from there to the mill. He set Jill loose on the town's shops, while he procured a nice hotel room as well as some snacks and refreshments for that afternoon. After a short time, he caught up with Jill and the two headed for their Mill.

Jill was bubbling about all of the shops. David tried to ignore her comment. He had long since discovered that when women get on a shopping binge, it is best to just ignore them. When she told him she found a restaurant named Quincey's that had a prime rib special for all you can eat of prime ribs and trimmings for twelve dollars a person, his ears perked up.

"Say, Jill that prime rib joint sounds right up my alley. What do you think?"

"Well, I expected you to say that, my meat and potatoes guy," she laughed.

"David, what is in the cooler in the back seat?"

"Oh, I got it to keep our lunch and drinks in for tomorrow I thought we might picnic at the house tomorrow. I will pick up ice and stuff to go in it while you get yourself together in the morning."

"That is great, but why did you say get myself together?"

"Well, I am just saying, I have noticed sometimes it takes you a bit of time in the mornings," he commented.

"OK, David. You do the grocery shopping in the morning, my love."

In about twenty minutes they were back at Mill Creek Road. Soon they had their gate open and were driving in to the house. David commented that the next day they must try and meet with the caretaker and also perhaps the two neighbors they shared Mill Creek Road with. Jill wholeheartedly agreed with that. They parked at the house and went in again to what was now truly theirs.

"Let's start a list of furnishings. We can prioritize it into 'must have immediately' and 'need later'. What do you think?" she asked.

"Sounds like a plan," David responded.

As the pair walked from room to room, filling up several pads of paper with their lengthy list of furnishings, it was soon after 5 o'clock. David was the first to say he was getting hungry. Jill on the other hand was still going strong, but agreed she didn't want her fellow to starve. They agreed to have Mexican fare that night, saving Quincey's for the next night.

12. A Proposal

As he tried to sleep that night, without much success, David thought back on all of all the excitement that day. His mind reminisced back over the past two years that led to the conclusion of their great search. He thought about the past day, how great it had been, even down to the Mexican dinner they had that night. But it wasn't having eaten too much Mexican food that kept David from sleep. No, it was what lay ahead for the coming day.

David had rehearsed it so many times in his mind over the past two years. It should have been easy, but it wasn't. He was quite nervous. He knew he would have but one opportunity to get it right. It just had to be perfect. What if she said no? Or if she waffled, saying she wasn't ready. The worries piled up on David.

It had to be tomorrow. They were flying back the following day on Sunday. What was the weather forecast? What if it were cold or rainy? Everything just had to be perfect, he kept telling

himself. Finally, he dozed off for just a bit of sleep before he was awakened by Jill.

"Wake up. Usually, you are the one getting me up. Are you ok?" she asked.

"Yes, I am fine. What time is it, Miss Sunshine? Guess I have overslept."

"Well, it is after eight. We have a lot to do today so rise and shine. Let's go!"

As David showered, he ran through in his mind one more time his plans for the day. He had called Tim the night before to make sure he could come out to the mill for a morning meeting at 10:30. That was the only 'must do' item for the day. It would leave the afternoon open for staging his big event.

David quickly dressed while leaving Jill to shower and get ready. He headed out early visiting a deli for their lunch sandwiches and a flower shop for a small bouquet of flowers which he concealed in the vehicle. When he picked up Jill at their hotel, she asked what he had in the cooler?

He commented, "You will have to wait until we get to the house to find out."

"Is Micky D's good for you for a bit of breakfast this morning, before we head to the house?" David asked.

"Sure, that will be fine. I am still full from too much Mexican last night," she commented.

David's worry about the weather spoiling his plans for the day now looked remote. At the moment it was a beautifully chilly mountain morning. Very invigorating, both agreed. David had carefully laid in provisions for their lunch at the house and celebratory hors d'oeuvres for later.

Tim Hargrove showed up right on schedule at 10:30.

"Hi, I am Tim Hargrove, we spoke by phone last night.

I believe you said you are David Mack, is that correct? And who might this young lady be?"

"Welcome Tim, yes, we spoke last night. I am David Mack. This is my good friend and half Old Mill owner, Jill Howard," David responded. "Tim, Bill told me you had been here for some time, by chance did you ever know my Uncle Henry?"

"Yes, I certainly had the pleasure of knowing him a few years before his unfortunate death. Based on your age, I suspect you never met Henry. Let me tell you about how I met that special man.

"It was, I think, 1995 or 1996, can't remember which. I was working as a carpentry foreman for a contractor in Leadville. My boss had contracted with Henry to build this house here. As it turned out, I worked closely with Henry on the design and construction of the building. I had a great respect for your uncle. He was not one to cut corners. He expected quality work. I can assure you that you have a well-built house here, even though it is now over twenty years old.

"Henry and I became close. He was devastated by his fiancé's death. You know he was building this house as a surprise for her. They were to live here in their later years. I tried to help keep his spirits up those last two years. He made me promise to look after the place. Bill and I have been doing so ever since.

"Henry was a really grand landscape painter. He gave me a couple of his paintings. I often asked him to paint this wonderful old mill. He curiously told me he had done two paintings of it which he was leaving for two special people.

It was always a mystery to me why he never wanted to talk about painting this special place."

"That is wonderful that you thought so much of my great Uncle Henry. From all I have heard about him, he must have been quite unique. I would like to tell you about those two mill paintings he mentioned to you. Jill and I have both of them. You see, they brought us together and led us here. I am sure that sounds a bit unbelievable. You know that Henry was my great uncle. So, my painting came to me through my father.

"Jill here just happens to be a relative of Henry's Carolyn. Henry left a part of a message on the back of each painting, setting forth a challenge for solving the riddle of the two paintings and finding the Old Mill. Like Henry told you, those paintings were special," David said.

"I am so glad that a relative of Henry has come forward. Do you plan to keep the place? I hope."

"We sure do," David responded. "Since Jill and I presently live in Georgia we have not decided just how much we can use the place. We also have another year of school to finish. But we are definitely going to hang on to it.

"Tim, we understand Mr. Brooks hired you to help him look after and maintain the property. Jill and I wanted to meet you and see if there is any way we could hire you to look after it, especially for the next year, until we graduate. Would you be able to help us?" David asked.

"Sure, I would be glad to. I am sure Bill told you my wife and I had to move back to town due to her health issues. I could come out here a couple of days a week to check things out and do what's needed, if you like."

"That will be fine, one other thing, we may be getting some furnishings for the house delivered and may need for you to receive them. We could coordinate times with you," David added.

"I will be glad to take care of that for you as well," Tim said.

"Tim, before you go, maybe you could answer a few questions about the compound. For example, what is the source of water for the house. We noticed the water is apparently turned off."

"That's right. I haven't had it on in the main house for quite some time. I will need to get the water turned on for you and check that all the fixtures work ok. It generally should be turned off and drained over the winter when no one is using the house. You know, because of the pipes freezing. As for the source there is a well located between the main house and the cabin. We have always had a good supply of great ice-cold water.

"Both the main house and the cabin are on a septic system. That has always worked great, though it has never been used for the added capacity of the main house. It should be fine as well.

"Bill has had me do a bit of maintenance on both the main house and the cabin's exteriors to keep them from deteriorating. About a year ago, we replaced the exposed decking on the main house, re-chinked, and stained the log exterior. Any other maintenance you need, I will be glad to help you with," Tim offered. "As you may know, I presently am working for a contractor in Leadville. David and Jill, have you two been able to get over to Leadville yet?"

"Sure have. We are staying in the Mountain Mine Hotel. And yes, we have discovered the Prime Rib's special at Quincy's. We plan to eat there tonight," David commented.

"Well, you have discovered the best meal in Leadville. Sounds like you two are settling into mountain life pretty good. Nice to meet both of you and look forward to seeing a lot more of you. Sometime you must meet my son, Ben. He is about your age I believe," Tim said as he was leaving.

With everything settled with Tim, the pair continued discussing furnishing the house as they enjoyed their picnic lunch on the lone round table on their porch. David intentionally stretched out their lunch until after 1 o'clock. He was still very nervous and even suggested an unusual glass of wine with lunch to settle his nerves.

Finally, the time had arrived. He thought this is it. *For better or worse I just have to do it. I must ask her.*

"Jill how about we walk down to the Old Mill again? I want to get a few more pictures," he suggested.

"Sure, I would love to."

With that the two went down the steps from the back deck, walking holding hands. They followed the stone path down to the mill. At the mill platform, they stood there looking at the rushing stream pounding against the timbers and pilings supporting one side of the mill. David positioned Jill just right, in order to get the perfect picture of her with the mill and the stream. He reached behind a bush and produced his bouquet for her to hold while he took her picture.

"Say where did you get the beautiful flowers? Oh, how sweet!"

"Now let me take your picture," she insisted. "Don't act so nervous, your hands are shaking. Really, I am not going to push you in the water and freeze you," she promised.

David thought to himself, I must calm down, she even noticed that I am nervous. This is so embarrassing.

Just then, the sun burst forth from behind a cloud, fully illuminating the mill and making the water sparkle. Taking that as his cue David, again somewhat shaky, dropped to one knee, like he had seen in the movies. He pulled the ring box from his pocket.

"David, what are you doing?"

"Jill, I do love you so. I can think of nothing more grand than to spend my life with you. Will you consider being my wife?"

"Yes! O yes! Why did you wait so long to ask me? I have been in love with you ever since we first met. Couldn't you tell? Guess, we had to find our Old Mill first."

"Oh, I am thrilled you said yes! I was scared you wouldn't," he said.

"So, that was why you were so nervous and this is why you wanted wine at lunch. You foolish guy, couldn't you tell I was madly in love with you!"

David stood up and embraced her. Then he quipped, "As for the delay, as you said, we had to find the perfect spot. I knew from that night in Gatlinburg, watching you sleep in my arms as the fire died out, that I would ask you to marry me one day. You look beautiful even when you are asleep. It has been frightfully hard waiting for this day. You, saying yes, has made this the happiest day of my life. I do love you so!"

"Well, we did find the perfect spot, didn't we."

With that, there was a long embrace with no small amount of passionate kissing. He then showed her the ring, saying I hope it is the right size as she lovingly placed it on her ring finger, assuring him it fit perfectly.

"Come, let's get back up to the house. I have some champagne on ice!" David announced.

"So that was what was in the cooler." Jill kidded David, "You, sure seemed nervous proposing, what with your hands shaking so. Are you sure you don't need me to pop the cork on the champagne bottle?"

"No, I can manage just fine, and please don't kid me about that. I never asked a girl to marry me before, ok. Hope I don't have to again."

"I hope you don't have to either, my love," she said with a big smile.

While consuming their liquid refreshments and snacks, Jill remembered the gifts Bill had given them.

"Let's open Bill's gifts," she said.

"Sure, you can open yours. we are drinking mine," he said while toasting her again with his glass of bubbly.

"So, Bill gave you champagne? How did you know?"

"Well, let's just say, your intended is just a little smarter than the average bear," David smugly commented. "Now let's see what he gave you."

They had left the large gift as well as their two paintings at the mill the previous afternoon. David quickly retrieved Jill's large wrapped package.

"OK dear, open it up and let us see what Bill gave you."

Soon Jill revealed a beautiful custom carved sign with engraved lettering. It read: WELCOME TO THE OLD MILL David and Jill Mack.

"You are kidding! He knew we were getting married," she shouted. "You told him? You dog."

"Well, I had to tell him something when I asked him to get the champagne, didn't I? I about died when he made that comment yesterday about marriage. I was afraid he was going to give it away"

"So that is why you had that coughing fit, like you were going to die. How funny!"

Soon they started making all sorts of plans, beginning with plans for a wedding.

"I guess Jill we need to decide when and where we might want to do this thing called a wedding," David said lightheartedly.

"You are right, we probably should wait until we graduate in May, don't you think?" she asked.

"That makes sense. We will be waiting almost a year though," he bemoaned.

"Yes, but we will have something grand to look forward to. Besides it will take some time to plan for…." At this point they both simultaneously said, "A wedding here at the Old Mill House!"

"So, we agree it has to be here?" she asked.

"Sure do, wouldn't think of any other place. This is the perfect spot. Not sure all our family and friends will think so, but it is however, OUR wedding."

"You know Henry and Carolyn planned to wed here, it's

as though we are fulfilling their destiny don't you think?" Jill said.

"I sure do, and I am thrilled to be doing that," he said.

Being down in a valley beneath peaks looming above, the shadows of the late afternoon sun started to darken the house. That and the coolness of the air alerted them it was time to head back to their hotel in Leadville.

"Say, Jill, you sure that restaurant said, 'all you can eat about prime rib'? That sounds almost too good to be true. I am about ready to put them to the test," David bragged.

That night over dinner, while stuffing themselves on prime rib, they made plans for the next day. David wanted to stop by the house briefly to do some measuring of the rooms for a floor plan he was drawing. He felt a drawing might help them plan for furnishings. Jill was getting really excited about furnishing 'their Mill House'. They also started the discussion about how they were going to use the house and when.

After a last quick visit to the mill house, they headed back to Denver and the airport. Their plane was scheduled to leave at 12:30. On the flight back they discussed how to break all the news to their families. Jill speculated they would freak out. David agreed, she was probably right about that. They concluded only time would tell, but nothing would take away from their state of euphoric happiness. They could think of nothing but marriage and their wonderful Old Mill.

13. Spilling The Beans

During their return flight, the pair continued their discussion on how they were going to break all their news to their families. It helped that Jill's parents had already met David's parents and they all seemed to get along well. They decided to break all their news to each set of parents separately. First, they would meet with David's folks, then with Jill's.

Jill expressed one of her biggest fears would be how her parents would react to their potential move to Colorado. David agreed that his parents probably wouldn't care for that either. They reasoned that once they saw the property, they would likely be more accepting.

Since both sets of parents had, more or less, nine to five jobs, they would tell David's parents the night they arrived and tell Jill's the following evening. Rather than provide such shocking news in a restaurant setting, they had decided to have home cooked meals. David would invite Jill over the first night and the next night Jill would invite David over.

To put the 'springing of the news' plan in motion David had called his parents the night before and asked his mother if she wouldn't mind having dinner for Jill and him when they arrived back late Sunday afternoon before he took Jill home. David told her they should be there around 6 pm.

His parents were thrilled to have them. On the drive from the airport to his parent's house, David looked over at Jill and asked, "You nervous? Ready for whatever happens? It will probably be a dinner to remember!" he teased her.

"Stop David, now you are making me nervous."

David's father greeted them, "Come on in you two, have a seat in the den. Alice is just finishing up with dinner. She will join us soon. How was your flight?"

"Oh, it was fine. Sorry for the quick notice about dinner," David said.

Jill offered, "Is there anything I can do to help?"

"No thanks, we have everything ready, I even have the table set, though Alice always gets on me about how I set it. Can I get you, almost legal young adults, a beverage?" Brad asked.

David spoke up, "Dad if you don't mind, I could stand a glass of white wine and I believe Jill might like one as well."

"Sure, that will be fine," David's father responded.

They had a half a glass worth of small talk before his mother Alice, called everyone into the dining room for dinner.

"Mrs. Mack, I mean Alice, thanks for having me over for dinner tonight. I know it was such short notice."

"No problem at all, dear. We are just happy to have both of you and are anxious to hear all about your trip," Alice said.

"That is so nice of you. David and I were very anxious to share the news of our trip with both of you. I will share our best news first. Your son has asked me to marry him and I was so excited to say yes. I do love him so," Jill gushed forth.

"Well congratulations to you both. I can't say this is too unexpected. It has been obvious for some time how much you love each other, and how alike you two are. You two are such a great match," Alice said.

Brad toasted them saying, "May you two have a wonderful, loved filled life."

David continued, "That is only a part of our exciting news. Let me now tell you the rest. Simply .... we finally solved the riddle of the Old Mill paintings."

Jill piped up, "Boy did we ever solve it!"

"Mom and Dad, I know this will all be hard for you to believe or accept. Great Uncle Henry planned for Jill and I to use his two paintings to find each other and the Old Mill. We did. We found it. Uncle Henry planned all that has happened before he died. Dad, you and I got one of the mill paintings, and Jill's mother and Jill got the other, each with half of the note. By solving his amazing puzzle, we now actually own the Old Mill, just as the note promised!"

"What do you mean you own it?" Brad questioned.

"This last trip was to sign the ownership papers. Now Jill and I own the Old Mill and the one-hundred-acre property that goes with it. The mill property is located in Colorado near the town of Leadville."

"It seems that Mr. Bill Brooks, the executor of Henry's estate, had been expecting us for quite some time. Again, the reason for our recent trip was to sign the paperwork. The mill property consists not only of the mill but also a large home Henry built shortly before he died. The property totals about one hundred acres and even has an old gold mine on it.

"There is one more thing, in addition to the wonderful property he also left us a large amount of money. Yes, his Will gave us the amount of nearly one and one half a million dollars," David announced.

"David, this can't be true. Are you sure this is not just some hoax? I want to see what you signed," Brad insisted.

"Jill, have you told your parents about your engagement and about the Old Mill?" Alice asked.

David piped up, "No, really, it is all true. We even met the Old Mill's caretaker who had known Henry. His story matched what Bill Brooks told us, all which is confirmed by our research."

Jill, then responded, "We intend to tell my parents all our news tomorrow night. You are the first ones we have told about this."

"I know this is very shocking. It certainly was for us, to think we own such a place out in Colorado and have a million and a half dollars before we even graduate from college. It is a lot to take in."

"You are sure right about that, this is a lot to take in!" his mother said.

"One more thing, we would like to have our wedding at our Old Mill House next June, after graduation. Now let us show you pictures of our spread," David bragged.

The two then showed his parents the multitude of pictures they had taken in Colorado, including the one he took of Jill before he proposed to her. He also showed his parents a copy of the deed to the property as well as a copy of Henry's Will. His parents just kept shaking their heads in disbelief that such an outlandish thing had happened. His mother, as well as Jill, were crying with emotion.

Alone, while driving Jill back to her apartment, David commented, "That went well don't you think?"

Jill laughed, "Oh you think that? I believe your parents think us both crazy! And still, it went well? I can only imagine how my parents will react tomorrow night. I will need a sleeping pill tonight and a lot of wine with dinner tomorrow night."

"I'll drink to that," David joked.

David was to arrive at Jill's parent's house at seven o'clock. He was right on time. When Jill answered the door, he quietly asked her, "Have you let the cat out of the bag yet?"

His pert lass responded, "No, Mister Mittens is resting on his cat tree."

"Boy, am I nervous," David commented.

"Don't be. They like you and they will just take it all in," she said.

"Hello David, good to see you again. Hope you brought your appetite," Jill's father greeted him.

"I sure did, Sir," David responded.

"Here now, there will be none of that Sir stuff. You must call us by our first names Jason and Mary," her father reminded him.

In a replay of the previous evening, Jill begged her folks

to serve white wine before dinner. She waited until her parents had consumed half a glass of wine each while she and David had downed a full pour. As they were ready to sit down to eat, Jill sprung her news about their engagement.

"So, you two had to go all the way to Colorado to get engaged. Guess Georgia just wasn't romantic enough, huh? Well congratulations, Jill and David," her father said.

"Sweetheart, I can't see how you could have found a better life partner than David," Jill's mother added. Then as the previous night, there was a wine glass toast.

"To our wonderful daughter and our soon to be son-in -law, David. May you two have all the happiness in the world," her father said.

Jill then spoke up, "We have a lot more news. David why don't you tell them our other news."

"OK, yes, we have had an exciting two trips to Colorado recently. I know you may have wondered why we went out there twice. The amazing truth is we finally solved the mystery of the two old mill paintings and the cryptic notes on the back of the paintings."

Jill again piped up, "Boy did we ever!"

"Do you want to take over here, dear, or shall I continue?"

"Oh no, you continue," Jill said.

"Well, our research led us to an attorney in Denver who was the executor of Henry Mack's (the paintings artist) estate. Astonishingly, Henry Mack (my great uncle) set this whole painting thing up as a game to get Jill and I together, and to end up giving us everything. The story we were told by the attorney who was Henry's executor was this: Henry was very much in love with Jill's great aunt Carolyn. They got engaged shortly before she suddenly passed away after an accident. The larger painting of the Old Mill was painted as a surprise for her. Upon her death, you ended up with it. After her untimely death, Henry painted the smaller old mill painting and had his executor see that David's father got it. Apparently, Henry wanted Jill and I to find each other and to have what he had wanted to share with his love, Carolyn. He wanted us to have what her death prevented him from having.

"He wanted young relatives of himself and Carolyn to inherit his property, all of it. And so as shocking as it sounds, that is exactly what has happened. Jill and I now jointly own the hundred-acre property containing the old grist mill, a large modern home, and even an old gold mine. If that was not enough, he also left us a sum of money, about one and one half a million dollars!"

"Is this some kind of a joke?" Jason asked.

Jill spoke up, "No, dad and mom, this is no joke, we really have it all. We have the deed. We have verified it all, have visited the property several times, and have pictures to show you. Oh, and we want to have our wedding there at our Old Mill House next June."

Mary said, "I am speechless, how could this have happened?"

They both expressed interest in seeing the property and finding out just what the pair had gotten themselves into. Jason formalized it by asking, "When can we come out with you to see your Old Mill?"

14. Cleaning, Repairing & Furnishing

Needless to say, their new found wealth in Colorado affected the pairs plans for the remainder of that summer. Instead of full-time jobs as they had planned, David and Jill decided to spend their time in Colorado getting the Mill House in order. It needed to be cleaned, repaired, furnished, and prepared for guests. All that needed to be done before school started back in the Fall.

It was imperative to accomplish these things in order to have a chance of it being ready for the wedding, scheduled to occur soon after they graduated. Once classes started in the Fall, they knew quite well they wouldn't have the time.

Their plan was to drive David's SUV out on July 21st, spend three weeks there, then drive back. They were aware that both of their families were anxious to see just what their kids had gotten themselves into. Both sets of parents wanted to visit ASAP. It was setting up to be a fun, but very hectic three weeks.

While David and Jill were anxious to show the place off, they wanted to spend at least a week out there by themselves doing some of the basic cleaning. They wanted to get some furniture delivered and arranged before starting to entertain family. David, being the planner of the two, worked out a preliminary schedule that would give both sets of parents several days at what they now termed 'Mill House'. Jill thought they could put their families to work on the house if the pair hadn't finished by the time they arrived.

As a precursor to ordering furniture, David had attempted to sketch a floor plan of the Mill House. He felt his plans were lacking. He did have an idea though. He thought that since Tim had worked on the building of the house, he just might have a set of the original plans. David was correct. Tim did have plans. He sent them to him. In addition, he forwarded pictures he had taken in the various rooms. This information supplemented that already prepared by David.

In the meantime, Jill was like a little girl with her first dollhouse. She had purchased a home CAD software program for her computer and had programmed the house plans so she could play with furniture arrangements.

With Tim's plans and pictures, they were set to order some of the basic furnishings. Getting them delivered was another matter, however.

David was busy trying to figure where they could get furniture and how it could get delivered to backwoods Colorado. He needed to get at least a few essentials such as beds so he and Jill could rough it in the house. He finally concluded that, in order to get beds there in time, David would have to rent a truck and go to either Colorado

Springs or Denver to pick them up. Once he had them, he would have to get Tim or Ben to come over and help him unload and get them upstairs.

In the days since arrival back at the Mill House, while searching for furniture they were staying at the hotel in Leadville. It was during this time that David indulged his curiosity to thoroughly explore the Old Mill. Other than a couple of peeks he had not really been all through the main mill or the original mill operator's quarters. He asked if Jill wanted to join him. She had responded she wanted him to check it out first. She feared the cobwebs and rodents.

As David investigated the machinery, it all appeared very old. He observed the lever and rusty metal gears that engaged the horizontal drive shaft. There was a leather belt with pulleys that transferred motion to an ancient looking dynamo. He observed some of the parts seemed to have been replaced. At the time, the dynamo was not engaged to produce power. He surmised the lights were fed off public power.

David then moved thru a door into the mill operator's quarters. There he discovered three rooms. There was a storage room, a kitchen with an old wood fired cook stove, and a bedroom with two bunks for sleeping. Immediately, he got the idea of spending the night in the extremely rustic and scary quarters.

David knew it would be a tough sell to get Jill to join him in this adventure. He was determined. On his next trip to town, he would buy a couple of sleeping bags and air mattresses. Then after a bit of clean-up of the space and after plying her with wine, he hoped to get her to keep him company there for a night.

As he had imagined, she was less than enthused with the idea. With a bit more wine and more pleading, she agreed. After having reheated take-out pizza that night they took their flashlights and a DVD to play on David's laptop computer and headed down to the mill. He had already swept it out and blown up the mattresses and laid out the sleeping bags on the bunks.

All was well at first. They watched a movie, not the scary one he considered. Soon after the movie concluded, they were lulled to sleep by the sound of rushing water beneath them. It was three in the morning when David was awakened by a noise. He lay there trying to determine what it might be. It wasn't long before Jill's shriek confirmed his suspicion. It had been a mouse. She declared that would be her last night sleeping there.

As they were beginning to think visiting family might have to stay in a hotel in Leadville until they got the house in order, they got good news. Finally on July 25th David had located beds and dressers in stock at a furniture store in Colorado Springs. As for beds, they were going for a king sized in the master bedroom, queens in two upstairs bedrooms and two twin beds in the third upstairs bedroom.

He and Jill would pick up a rental truck the morning of the 26th and drive over to Colorado Springs to get a load. In the meantime, Jill had ordered sheets, bedspreads, and towels thru Amazon, which were to be delivered on the 27th. All seemed to be planned out.

Tim showed up at 7 am on the 27th to help David unload the truck and get the furniture upstairs. As soon as that was accomplished, Jill followed David to return the rental truck. With the arrival of the linens later that day, the pair could finally start setting up bedrooms. This was only two days before the first family members were to arrive. Despite all the many tasks to accomplish, David and Jill worked in harmony with their goal of proudly showing off their new home to their loved ones.

The big items remaining were sofas and chairs for the Great Room and Dining Room table and chairs. Jill had ordered those from a furniture showroom in Denver and had paid the extra freight charge to have those items delivered by the 30th.

As for their families; David's parents were due to arrive on the 29th for four days and Jill's folks were coming on Aug. 4th for four days. It was obvious that due to some furnishings arrivals, the house would not be completely furnished for the visits. The young couple felt that it would be livable however.

One stroke of good luck was that they had ordered appliances and Tim had received them and had them installed before David and Jill got to Colorado. Jill, for her part, was constantly on Amazon ordering an assortment of things from small tables to small appliances, such as a coffee maker. She had even ordered things such as dishes and glasses that way. David was concerned with how much might get broken in shipment. Jill had great confidence in Amazon.

Once the kitchen things had arrived, Jill undertook the task of setting up her kitchen. She undertook this task with pride, arranging everything just to her liking, in spite of David's helpful suggestions of where to place things. By the 29th she had it to her liking and was ready to start preparing meals.

"I am ready to cook! But we have no food. Must go to the grocery," Jill exclaimed.

Another large Amazon arrival that David was anxiously awaiting was the furniture for their deck. David felt properly furnishing the deck was vital. He wanted everyone to be able to just sit and take in the view. The view of the stream tumbling over the rocks. The view of the not so distant snow covered peaks framed by their forest. The view of their quaint Old Mill with its turning water wheel.

And finally enjoy the sounds of the stream and the swishing sound the water- wheel made. As for other senses, there was the wonderful smells of nature.

There was one other thought the couple had discussed while sitting out on their deck. It was still rather cool. They considered that in all likelihood it would be like that a lot of times. Quickly they determined to order a propane fueled, tower radiant heater, once again from good old Amazon. Hopefully he would remember to pick up propane for it, David thought.

Though it was summer, it still got cold in the evenings so they decided to have a fire in their Great Room fireplace. For that they would need some firewood. Again, with his usual thoughtfulness Tim was on it. He brought them a pickup load of split wood. David thanked him and said in the future he planned to buy a chain saw and split his own wood.

While taking one last break before his parent's arrival, David commented, "You know, Jill, it is sure a good thing

Uncle Henry left us a pile of money because we have certainly spent a shit load in the past couple of weeks."

"Yes, you are right, but I don't think we have been wasteful. I feel he would approve of our furnishing of his home, don't you?" she asked.

"I do. Despite the work, I have enjoyed making this our home," David added.

David's mother and father had rented a car at the Denver airport for the drive to the Old Mill. As they neared Mill Creek Road, David gave them directions by cell phone so that they did not miss the turn-off. They arrived at 3 o'clock that afternoon of July 29th. Jill told David he wanted him to also give her parents directions by phone when they arrived since it had worked so well for his parents.

"Well son, we finally made it. Great to see you both. What a remote spot and such a large log house. Where is this Old Mill? I don't see it," his father exclaimed.

"You will. Let us show you the house," Jill offered.

As they entered the Foyer, David proudly pointed out one of their Old Mill paintings hanging on the wall, saying "there is the Old Mill". The wall was blocking the view of the Great Room and the real Old Mill.

"OK Son, I mean the real mill, we have seen the painting before," his dad commented.

Jill admonished him, "David, do bring them on in here, stop with the games."

"Wow, this room is so grand and the view out back. Oh, there is the real Old Mill," his mother exclaimed.

Jill commented, "Let us show you around, then you can

freshen up before we have some wine and hors d'oeuvres out on the deck."

"That sounds grand, dear," Mary commented.

Soon David's dad returned and wanted to go down and see the mill. David was quick to oblige while Jill remained up at the house getting snacks and drinks for the foursome. Brad, being the engineer, was very curious about the mill's operation. He questioned how much power it might produce. David explained that presently the house was powered by the public electric service but that he had the mill powering lighting at night as well as the caretakers cabin.

Brad expressed suspicion that the now old dynamo would probably not be able to provide their entire needs. He also suggested that retrofitting the mill with a new one might not be practical. Enough negativity, David thought.

Brad and Mary spent their visit looking for things to help with, such as setting up the dining room furniture that arrived while they were there. They also took note of anything the pair might need and started ordering accessories while there. All in all, it was a good, but slightly exhausting visit.

As soon as David's folks left, the pair set about preparing the house for her parents who were due the next day. By the time her parents arrived, all the furniture was in place and they felt the house looked really good. Jill was anxious that her parents would approve.

"So dear, David gave us excellent directions and had our flight not have been delayed we would have been here a might sooner," her mom said.

"Mom and dad, I will show you around, and David why don't you put their luggage in their room, dear."

David quickly obliged. After having been shown the house, Old Mill, and cottage, Jason's response was, "David and Jill you need a security system for this place." David felt this was unnecessary but Jason had his mind set on it and by days end he had arranged for a Colorado Springs security company to send out technicians the next day with cameras and security devices. In addition, he had the company bring and install an automated security gate for the property's entry.

David and Jill graciously thanked her parents for what they thought was an unnecessary expense. The next day, Mary was interested in going into Leadville to survey the florist shops there. She had already formulated her ideas as to floral arrangements for the upcoming wedding the next year. She wanted to confirm that the local florist might be able to provide their needs.

For her part, Jill was a bit mortified and afraid that her mother being a florist, might create friction with the local florist. David told Jill he believed he would let her accompany her mother while he and Jason stayed and dealt with the security system. Her response to him was "gee thanks".

As for the security system, Jason was to spare no expense to get them 'everything he felt they needed' which included six cameras for the compound, an alarm system for the main house as well as the cabin, and down to thermostats they could control from their I-phones. David just shook his head at the ten thousand dollars spent. Fortunately, it was a gift from Jason and Mary.

By the time Jill's parents left, the couple was completely exhausted. They stayed one extra day just to rest before returning to Atlanta.

15. The Phone Call – History Repeated?

Shortly after returning from their marathon three-week trip to Colorado, the pair were attempting to get back into their senior year in college. It had been a busy summer and looked to be a tough last year in school as well. Jill was to receive her bachelor in education with a minor in creative writing. David, on the other hand, would be getting a bachelor in building science.

As one more activity for the new home owner's, the pair decided to attend the Fall Home Show at the Civic Center. Neither had ever been to one but since they were now home owners, they were anxious to see what the show was about. The Home Show was on a Saturday. Normally David would have picked up Jill at her apartment but that Saturday she had a bridal shower for a friend. The shower was being held near the Civic Center.

Obviously, David had no interest in attending a bridal shower and Jill did not know how soon she could get away so they planned to communicate by cell phone. Jill had hoped to get away by 11:30 and they would meet at a downtown restaurant for lunch before going to the home show. Expecting her to be at the restaurant no later than noon, David planned to get there early and reserve a table.

Right on schedule, Jill called at 11:30 telling him she was departing the shower and would see him soon. Noon rolled around and she had not shown. He tried to call, assuming she was in traffic. David waited until 12:30 still no Jill, or calls. He then began to panic. He called the showers hostess, who confirmed that Jill left at 11:30.

David knew Jill's roommate was out of town so calling her would be of no use. Finally, about 1 o'clock, in desperation, he decided to call the flower shop to see if her mother had heard from Jill. He asked for Mary Howard. The clerk answering the phone said she was not there at present. She said Mrs. Howard had to leave suddenly on a family emergency. At that point, David told her who he was. He told her he was trying to reach Jill.

The clerk told him she understood Jill had been in an accident and was taken to the hospital. David asked the woman, which hospital? The clerk said she wasn't sure. He then decided to try and call Jill's mother's cell phone. It was busy. Not unexpected under the circumstance, he thought. He would have to keep trying.

Before he tried to call again his cell rang. It was Jill's dad. He said that Jill had been in a car accident and was at Eastside Hospital in the ER. He went on to say the doctors had yet to tell he and Mary her condition but felt that he would want to know. David thanked him for the call and said he would come there immediately.

When David arrived at the hospital, he found Jill's parents in the ER waiting room.

"How is she? What happened?" He pleaded to know.

Jill's father being the slightly less distraught of the pair responded, "She has gone for an MRI presently. Hopefully the doctor will give us a report soon. What we do know is, presently she is unconscious. She was in a bad wreck on the expressway."

David said, "I spoke to her only two hours ago. She called me to say she was leaving the bridal shower and that she would be to the restaurant by noon. When she didn't show, I felt something awful might have happened."

About that time, the ER doctor showed up accompanied with a neurologist. The ER doctor introduced the neurologist, a Dr. Krisp. The doctor said their main concern was that she had suffered a cerebral concussion in the wreck. There was some swelling that showed up in the MRI. It was too early to tell just how much damage had been done. For the sake of allowing the brain to heal, they were going to keep her in an induced coma for a day or two. Only when they brought her out of that would they know if there would be damage. On an encouraging note, he said he had seen a number of such cases and he felt she might suffer no lasting impairment.

The neurologist said she was being moved to intensive care for the next day or so to make sure her vitals were carefully monitored.

After the report, they all thanked the doctors and asked when they could see her? The neurologist said presently she was getting stabilized in the ICU and they could have a brief visit in an hour. He reminded them she would be unconscious for some time. While the three waited for their brief visitation, they prayed.

David couldn't help but wonder if he was to be stricken with the same fate as Henry with Carolyn at the mill. Oh, how similar this seemed. Two fiancés dying of an accidental head injury. He must put that thought out of his head, he just must. She just couldn't die on him.

She looked rather better than he expected. Other than a bandage on her head, a neck collar, and a bunch of tubes and monitors she looked ok. Jill's mother was weeping and most distraught. David was trying his best to contain his emotions, but becoming unable to, he soon excused himself, telling her parents he would return the first thing in the morning.

For David it was a sleepless night. He felt guilty about not staying at the hospital. Emotionally, he just couldn't. He earnestly prayed she would recover and be ok. The next morning before going back to the hospital, he called his parents and gave them the news about Jill. They were likewise quite concerned and wanted to come to the hospital, He told them to let him go there first then he would update them.

David got back to the hospital early the next morning. Her parents were still there and shortly after he arrived, Janet arrived. This time she was in a more sedate mood, not acting the trouble maker she usually was. With his arrival, Jill's parents went home for a bit of rest. David was left alone with Janet and an unconscious Jill.

Janet tried to assure David that her sister would be alright, saying twins just know these things. The logic in that somehow escaped David. He did however feel it was a nice thing for her to say to him. He felt despite all the game playing she did, she really did like her sister a lot.

David said he was going to the vending machine to get a soft drink and offered to get Janet one. She thanked him saying she would like a diet Pepsi. He made a restroom stop, picked up the drinks, and was back in about 15 minutes. Immediately upon entering the room, he noticed the bed sheet was pulled up covering Jill's head. He lost it. He fully believed Jill was dead.

Then just as quickly, he realized she was still hooked up to all the monitoring. He uncovered her and as he did, she moved a bit. Still distraught, he hit the nurse-call button. About that time her prankster sister reappeared, acting innocent of the whole matter. David was very angry at her.

"Janet that was despicable of you. Believe me, that will not go unpunished," David promised.

Dr. Krisp told the family that Jill's vitals looked good and he was planning to have another MRI performed first thing the next morning. If the swelling had subsided, he might then be able to start bringing her out of the induced coma. The family was to be at the hospital by 9 am for the doctor to reveal Jill's status.

Unable to sleep, David showed up at the hospital at 7am. He asked the nurse if Dr. Krisp had come in yet? She said she thought he might have. She then said that he had been there late the night before and had performed another MRI on Jill. David then asked the nurse if she knew whether the doctor might have taken Jill off the medication to allow her to awake. She said he had. She was expecting the doctor to be by soon to check on her. David asked the nurse if he could possibly see her. The nurse told him that that would be fine.

As David entered Jill's room, he noticed the IV pump was off. A good sign he thought. He also noticed that she seemed restless and was moving about some. Another good sign, he thought. Finally, he decided to hold her hand gently and start trying to talk to her. Soon, to his astonishment, he could feel her squeezing his hand. Then it happened, she opened her wonderful eyes and though groggy, she was awake. David knew he probably should summon the nurse at once but he was so excited that he wanted to talk to Jill.

"David, where am I?" were the most wonderful words she had ever spoken to him. He leaned over and kissed her, dripping tears on her.

"You are fine, my love. You are in the hospital. You are going to be just fine," he told her she had been in a bad accident but was fine then. He went ahead and told her about Janet's prank making him believe she had died.

"That is even too sick for my sick sister," she said. "Let's do something equally mean to get even with my dear sister Janet. David, put your mind to a good plan for revenge. Now I need to call my parents and talk to them. They will be relieved to know I am awake. I also want to tell them how mean Janet was to you."

"Quickly, before you call, tell them we are going to play a prank on her and ask them to play along. I will explain my idea after your call. Better make your call short, Janet may show up soon and we need to plan," David said.

Following her speedy call, Jill asked David, "So what's your plan?"

"Well, I have two ideas. Since you had a potential brain injury, you can pretend not to recognize her. Another option would be for you to only speak French. You did take French, didn't you?

Wow, tough choice. I like both ideas. Let's go with selective amnesia. I will pretend not to recognize my twin. That should worry her a bit, don't you think?

"Sounds like a plan. Hope your parents play along," he commented.

Fortunately, Jill's parents arrived before Janet. As Jill explained the plan to them, David kept watch for Janet. As he saw her approaching, he stuck his head in the door to alert Jill and her parents. David then proceeded to tell Janet that Jill seemed okay, other than some memory issues.

Janet rushed to Jill's bedside. Rather than acknowledging her, Jill turned to David and quietly said, "David, I am sorry, but should I know her?"

Before David or Jill's parents could respond, a clearly shocked Janet said, "You recognized David, but not me, your sister? Mom, Dad, tell her I am her sister. Her twin," Janet, now in tears, pleaded.

Her parents remained silent.

"Surprise, how does it feel? Pretty bad? Perhaps no more thoughtless pranks, huh!" David said. By that point Janet was crying up a storm. David told her, "Jill is fine.

"Jill, I am so glad to see you. I did a really bad thing to

scare David like that, please forgive me. I am so, so glad you are okay," Janet said.

Her dad then said, "Janet, I am very disappointed in you. What you did to David was cruel and terrible. I really do hope this is the end of bad jokes on others, dear."

"It is dad, I swear," Janet said again, quite teary eyed.

Dr. Krisp reported that Jill's earlier swelling had subsided. In his opinion, she should make a full recovery. He did want her to remain in the hospital for another day so he could monitor her. He also cautioned against any heavy work for a week and no air travel where pressure changes could re-aggravate her brain swelling.

By the time Jill got out of the hospital, it was time for classes to begin again. What a summer it had been. They reminisced a few nights later at Casa Rustica while eating some good Italian food.

"You know, Jill, when you were laying there in the hospital I kept thinking about your aunt Carolyn and uncle Henry. I kept praying I wouldn't lose you as he lost the love of his life. Despite those painful thoughts I somehow knew you would be alright. You were too young and full of life to die. I felt my prayers would be answered. They were."

16. Wedding Planning

They had accomplished a great deal in Colorado during their three weeks visit the previous summer. Still, what remained were the final touches to the property. More importantly, making sure all the actual ceremony and reception items were lined up. All of this

necessitated another trip west over their final spring break.

First up would be a stop in Denver where Jill had elected to shop for her wedding dress. Her thinking was that she could pick out one there and have any alterations done there and pick it up on their return thru Denver prior to the wedding.

The pair had spent the night of April 16th in Kansas City and had hotel reservations the following night at a hotel in Denver. Dress shopping was set for the 17th.

"What do you mean I can't come with you? What am I to do for the next hour, or more likely hours?" David asked Jill.

"You know it is bad luck to see the bride in her dress before the wedding. We can't take any chances. You will just have to entertain yourself and I will call you when I am finished. You really should get a new suit for the wedding. On second thought, you had better wait and let me go with you to get a suit. I can only imagine what you might come up with," Jill commented.

By the time they finished shopping and ate lunch, it was the middle of the afternoon. They would need to hurry to get to the Mill House before dark. One concern David had was whether they would even be able to get into the house, due to remaining snow on their driveway. So far this would be the nearest to winter they had visited the mill property.

"Jill, cross your fingers our driveway is passable," David said as they prepared to turn in on Mill Creek Road.

"It sure better be, and I also hope Tim has the water to the house turned on as well," she responded.

"Just joking about the driveway. That was the reason your brilliant fiancé got a four-wheel drive SUV at the car rental place. As to the heat and water, I asked Tim to make sure the water was turned on last week and also to make sure the heat was working."

As they ventured down Mill Creek Road, it was covered in patches of lingering snow, the last which had only been a week earlier. David quickly engaged the four-wheel drive and they slowly made their way to the locked gate. He tried the gate code on his I-phone but the gate failed to open. Finally, he decided to get out and enter the code on the keypad. In the process, he stepped on an icy patch and promptly was on his butt. He could hear Jill laughing loudly.

Gate opened; they gingerly crossed a very icy bridge

over the creek. Finally, they were parked in front of their new home. Tim had cleared the snow from the front porch and steps, which was a blessing. David thought he must thank him for the extra effort.

"Home sweet home. And warm home," Jill commented, as they stepped inside.

"Pretty sweet," David said.

"You realize we are going to have to go out again right away, since we don't have anything to eat for dinner. I wonder if Quincey's is open this time of year? If not, how about a pizza?" David asked.

It was dark as they arrived back home after a good pizza dinner in Leadville. They had also stopped by a grocery to pick up supplies for their breakfast and lunch the next day. Soon the pair settled in for a romantic evening, with David building a fire in the master bedroom fireplace and splitting a bottle of wine before the crackling fire.

"So, wife-e, you going to make your man some good hardy breakfast vittles while he goes out to check out our estate?" David joked.

"No but I will kick your ass if you don't come and help me! And there will be no more of the wife-e business," Jill stated.

"Oh, I love it when you talk mean to me," he again joked.

Following a hearty breakfast, the two reviewed the list of appointments for the day. They planned to hit the caterer, florist, and the tent provider that day. The following day they were going to check with the two hotels, as well as the minister. Tim was also set to come by later that afternoon so they could discuss any arrangements they needed him to coordinate.

As one might expect, business was rather slow at both the florist as well as the caterer since tourist season had not begun. When they had finished at the florist and were leaving, David announced as they were getting into their vehicle, "You know I believe I laid my cellphone down in there. You stay in the SUV and I will go get it and be right back.

Back at the florist, David instructed her to add another six dozen white roses to their order. He said he would pick them up when he returned for the wedding. With their assigned tasks for the day accomplished, a hamburger lunch consumed, and more grocery shopping done, they returned home.

Tim arrived at 4 o'clock that afternoon. David had previously discussed with Tim about building a platform for the tent down by the old mill. The two walked down to pick a site while Jill prepared snacks and drinks for the three. David showed Tim the spot for the proposed deck. Unfortunately, there was still a patch of snow where it was to be placed.

Since the main purpose of the deck was to serve as a floor for the tent and David now had the tent size selected, he knew what size the deck should be. Tim said his son Ben could help him build it in a couple of weeks. The deck was to be 20 feet by 20 feet. The location was a relatively flat place, off to the side between the old mill and the cabin. With the possibility of keeping the deck after the wedding, David and Jill did not want it to take away the view of the mill.

Out of Jill's hearing, David spoke to Tim about another surprise project for the wedding.

David gave Tim a sketch he had prepared for a wooden entry arch. He wanted Tim to construct and erect it at the bridge. The lettering on the arch was to say 'THE OLD MILL' then below those letters 'David & Jill Mack'. He told Tim that he had ordered an additional six dozen white roses at the florists. He asked Tim to pick them up the day before they were to arrive back for the wedding and to use them to decorate the arched entry at the bridge. David wanted to surprise Jill with the arch and flowers when they returned.

Other than being a great surprise for Jill, he felt perhaps that would make up for the prank he planned to play on her, assuming it turned out badly. David had decided on a very risky prank to play on his bride to be. He started by finding the business card of the woman, in the Denver bridal shop, who had sold Jill her wedding dress.

A few days before the couple headed back to Denver, for the wedding at the Mill House, he called the sales clerk. He explained that he and Jill loved to play pranks on each other and he wanted to enlist her help in playing one on Jill. What David asked her to do was to see if she had a colored wedding dress, (the uglier the better), in Jill's size and have her name put on it. He added he would be there and try to capture Jill's reaction on video when she was presented with the wrong dress.

David said that after a moment of her initial shock he would tell her 'Just kidding' it was only a joke. The sales clerk finally agreed to go along, but warning David, "Mister, you are playing with fire. I hope she can take a joke and doesn't call off the wedding over this!"

David assured the nervous clerk that Jill could take a joke. Her concern, did however, give him pause.

17. An Old Mill Wedding

There was a surprisingly long list of invitees expected for a wedding in such a far-flung and remote place as the Old Mill in Colorado. Probably, curiosity over the strange location for a wedding is the reason many accepted. There were twelve from Jill's family, including her Colorado relatives. David had six family members. Then there were the Georgia friends, fifteen had accepted.

Others included Bill Brooks and his wife, as well as Tim and his wife and son. The special guest was to be Professor Murphy and his wife. All total, a group of forty was expected to invade the Old Mill. The couple also invited the Flanders, from North Carolina.

Most of the guest would be staying in hotels in Leadville. David and Jill had arranged very reasonable rates for them. After a lengthy discussion between the pair, it was decided that both sets of parents would stay in the main house in the days up until the wedding, then leave after the ceremony so David and Jill would have it to themselves that night.

Tim and his wife were hosting Bill and his wife at their home in Leadville. Professor Murphy and his wife would be staying in the nicest hotel in Leadville, compliments of David and Jill.

Before leaving Atlanta to prepare the final touches in Colorado, there was the bridal shower and bachelor party. Since most of Jill and David's friends and family were in Atlanta, it made sense to have both events there. Normally, both would be held within a couple of weeks of the wedding, but since the couple planned to head to Colorado right after graduation, they decided to have friends and family hold them the weekend before they drove west on Monday, May 27th.

Due to the timing restraints, Jill's bridal shower was to be on the same Saturday night as David's bachelor party. It seemed like a good scheduling solution. Since David was not quite as wild as some of his friends, it was expected, at least by Jill, that it would not be too raunchy. David's friend Bill had other plans, which included the participants attending a strip club show. And since they were all now of legal drinking age, alcohol was to figure heavily in the event.

One surprise guest attending David's bachelor party was Tim's son, Ben. He had asked if he could attend. This request seemed somewhat odd to David but certainly he didn't feel he could turn him away, especially if he was willing to fly all the way to Atlanta to attend.

In all, Jill was expecting about a dozen of her friends to attend her party and David, about nine at his. Bill, being his best man, took the lead in planning the bachelor party while Jill's mother and sister planned Jill's event. These parties were sort of secondary events when compared with their graduations and their travel west for the wedding.

"So, Jill, what fragrance of soap are they going to use on you in your shower?" David asked.

"Oh, I don't know, but I will probably have to use lye soap on you after you get dirty at your party. Perhaps I will need to wash your mouth out as well," she commented.

"No, I will be good, promise! And if there happen to be any strippers, I will just close my eyes," he said.

"Sure, you will! Bad David."

Their graduation was a large affair with over three thousand graduates in their class. Their proud parents took a bevy of photos of the two all dressed up in their caps and gowns. Jill's sister Janet was also in attendance. Since she took off a semester with the band, she wouldn't graduate until the end of the fall semester.

Then came the graduation parties. Both Jill's parents, as well as David's, held a large party for the couple at a nice restaurant. In addition to family, a number of their friends attended. An abundance of photos was taken at that event as well. After a 'bit' of wine, Janet asked Bill if it would be ok if she attended David's bachelor party the following Saturday night. Before Bill had a chance to respond, David gruffly stated, "Absolutely not, no offense though, dear future sister -in-law." All who heard the exchange laughed.

The Sunday morning after the bridal shower and bachelor party, Jill called David at 9 am. He was not awake, and being quite hung-over, he promised to come over midafternoon. When she saw David that afternoon at 3 o'clock, she could tell that David was in a bad way. He apologized for having drunk a bit too much at the party. Jill announced she was interested in seeing pictures of David's bachelor party. David grimaced, responding, "I have already deleted them."

After Jill provided a bit more coffee to David, the two completed the last-minute loading of his SUV and her car for their trip west the next morning.

"Say, David, my shower was great. Got a lot of swell gifts. We had a lot of fun playing games and drinking champagne. How was your stag party?" she again pried.

"Oh, it was ok, I guess. Only a little inappropriate. And yes, as you can tell, I did drink too much. I have a bad hangover today, but I will be fine for the drive tomorrow," David promised.

Jill commented, "One odd thing did happen at my shower. My normal party animal sister cut out early, after only about an hour. She joked she had a hot date. Jill said this seemed peculiar, even for Janet."

"That is strange. You know what is also strange, Ben also departed early from my bachelor party. And to think after flying all the way over here for it," David said. He then added, "You don't think?"

Before he finished his statement Jill piped up with, "Oh my gosh do you suppose they are dating?"

"Don't know, it is a mite curious though."

"They did sort of hit it off pretty well when they met out in Colorado," Jill responded.

"Well, that would explain why Ben was willing to fly all the way here for the bachelor party of someone he barely knows."

This trip west would be a bit lonely for the pair as this time they were each driving vehicles loaded to the brim with belongings and gifts. David insisted on leading their two-vehicle caravan. Though not actually together, their handsfree cell phones were put to good use with hours of conversations. The long trip would be broken up with an overnight stop in Kansas City.

They had been driving for three hours the next morning. Shortly after they crossed into Colorado, they made a stop at the state welcome center and rest area. Immediately, as he pulled in to park, David saw a very strange site. As David parked his SUV and Jill pulled in beside him, he heard her screaming.

"David, look at all those rabbits!" Jill shouted as they got out of their vehicles.

"That's cool, I have never seen so many rabbits," he commented.

"I wonder where they all came from and why so many are here.? Do you reckon a load of rabbits overturned? Are people here feeding them?" Jill asked.

David joked, "Don't know, but I bet people with dogs have their hands full when they stop here."

"Yes, lets watch for a few minutes and I want to get some pictures. No one will believe this scene. So many, they are everywhere," Jill said.

"Watch out you don't get mugged by rabbits in the restroom!" he joked.

Shortly after their rabbit rest stop, the pair pulled into an Arby's for lunch. While stopped, they reviewed their pictures taken at the rest stop. The picked out a couple of good ones to send to friends and family members. Each had fun offering up good captions for them.

Soon they were on the road to Denver. That afternoon, Jill was to pick up her gown that she had ordered in the spring. Following that, they had opted to spend the night in Denver. They would pick up a few items that weren't available in the smaller town of Leadville.

At the bridal shop, David was very excited to see the prank he had planned for Jill. Since he was not supposed to see her in the gown before the wedding, he was going to have to sneak into the shop after she went in. He had called their sales associate a couple of days earlier to make sure everything was set with the lavender colored dress, in lieu of the white gown Jill expected.

David's I-phone camera ready, the sales associate ushered him into the viewing area, as Jill took her wrapped dress to the changing room. It wasn't long before a shriek came from the dressing room.

"Ma'am, you gave me the wrong dress. Where is my white gown?" Jill pleaded.

"Isn't that the dress you ordered? It does have your name on it, doesn't it?" the sales lady asked.

"It may have my name on it but this sure as hell is not my dress! Where is my white wedding gown?" Jill again demanded.

David, while having a great time recording Jill's anguish, felt sorry for the clerk and so he popped out from behind a manikin and announced, "pranked you huh!"

"So, you think this is a good joke to play on me, mister. You may regret having done this!"

"Ma'am, I apologize to you for what my 'former' fiancé has had you do," Jill responded. After waving David out of the shop she tried on her correct dress and joined him out-side a short time later. Fortunately, by then, Jill had seem-ingly accepted his prank without any residual anger.

It was late morning the following day when David, this time successfully, used his I-phone to open the gate. As they started to drive into their new home, David motioned for Jill to drive in first. She stopped almost immediately. Just as the bridge came into view, she got out of her car with her phone in hand. It appeared she was intent on tak-ing a photo.

"David, what is this? Who put this marvelous entry arch up and the lovely white roses?" Jill asked.

"Don't know. You like it?" David asked.

"I love it. I must get a picture."

"Well, if you love it that must mean…I did it."

What David had designed and commissioned Tim to have made and install was a timber archway that one drove under at the approach to the bridge. The archway con-tained routed wood signage saying 'THE OLD MILL,' David & Jill Mack.

The scene Jill captured was quite spectacular. There was the beautiful roaring stream, the crisp green forest, still hid-ing patches of snow, and the cobalt blue sky above, making it perfect. Photographer Jill was soon busy documenting everything, including two deer that had been grazing near the cabin.

"Say dear, is it now or after the wedding I am supposed to tote you over the threshold?" David asked.

"First off you are not to TOTE me over the threshold, you are to carry me over, and it is traditional to do after the wedding I believe," she responded, then added, "Of course, if you need practice, you can carry me in now!"

"No, don't need practice, spec I can TOTE my 'old lady' when er it's time for the TOTING!" He again joked.

"Listen you, I not marrying some poor illiterate hillbilly, so straighten up!" She admonished him.

They soon confirmed that all appeared in order, just as they had left it, when they were last there two months earlier. It was getting dark as they completed the unloading. Both being tired and hungry, David suggested he could use a prime rib dinner. Jill agreed, so off to Leadville it was for a hearty meal for the pair. Arriving back at the Mill House around ten, they debated having a nightcap before bed.

"You know, we really shouldn't be sleeping in the same bed before the wedding," she joked.

"That ship has sailed. Get on over here. The house hasn't warmed up yet and I need some warmth."

"Yes love, happy to oblige!"

The next morning, they were up early. Jill began preparing breakfast while David checked out the cabin and turned the water on there. It was a blessing that Tim had come in a few days ago and turned the water on to the main house. Over breakfast they reviewed their list of the numerous chores that they had to accomplish over the next eleven days before the wedding.

The wedding was set for two o'clock on Friday, June 14th. Though it was eleven days until the actual wedding, it would only be six days before some family members and guests would be arriving. The reception that would follow there at the Mill House was to last until five and would include a small band and heavy hors d'oeuvres. They had decided on a western theme and had arranged for a professional chef to grill steaks for sandwiches on site.

First and foremost on Jill's mind was confirming that the catering was all set. Then she needed to check and ensure that the florist was all arranged. While Jill was to go into town the next day to meet with the florist and caterer, David was to follow up with Tim's son Ben, about the three-piece band he was arranging. Janet was going to sing for the wedding and wanted to also sing with the band for the reception. David was very nervous having her involved, due to his past history with her.

Additionally, David was to again meet with the minister to confirm both the wedding time and the date, time, and location of the rehearsal dinner. That was another task for David to verify with the restaurant the time and headcount for the rehearsal dinner. After making her rounds in Leadville, Jill was going to stop by the grocery and pick up a couple of steaks and baked potatoes for them to have on the grill that night. David was tasked with picking up some bottles of good wine.

"Don't forget to ask the caterer about supplying a bartender," David reminded Jill as she was preparing to leave for town.

They both returned later that afternoon. As Jill made salads, David marinated their steaks. He then set about getting the charcoal grill ready to cook on. Finally, he poured each a glass of chilled white wine.

"You do know, dear, we really should be drinking red wine with red meat," he commented.

"You can have red if you want but I am a white wine gal, in particular a Sauvignon Blanc gal. If you want red wine, you should be marrying Janet," she said.

"I'll drink to that," David said while toasting her.

In about forty-five minutes their dinner was ready. David had set the round table on the deck for their dining.

"I cannot imagine a more lovely spot to dine," Jill commented. "We have everything for the senses. The smell of the evergreens and wild flowers. The sound of our stream tumbling over the rocks and, of course, the view. It couldn't be more splendid."

"I agree with you completely, but for me there is one ingredient you failed to mention, that is sharing all this with someone you love."

"Hear, Hear!"

"How could anyone have a more splendid place for a wedding. This is just perfect. We are so very fortunate don't you think," Jill said.

"But as lovely as all this is, without you it could never be perfect for me. You are what makes my life perfect, now and forever," David said and leaned over to kiss her.

David had been anxiously watching the long-range weather forecast for the date of the big event. He had already learned from their numerous trips out there that the weather could change rapidly, therefore be very unpredictable. A week out it appeared as though they were to have fine weather, sunny with a high of upper sixties.

The Old Mill was down in somewhat of a valley, though being at a rather high elevation, it still got a bit chilly in the evening, once the sun began setting. Overnight, the temperature was hovering in the upper forties. Just good cool mountain weather. Great sleeping weather, as David put it. Jill agreed, though she had expressed some bit of concern about a sudden rain shower ruining their nuptials and reception party.

In an attempt to leave nothing to chance, David found a rental concern that would rent a medium sized pavilion tent. The company was to set it up on the deck Tim had built and have it ready if it did rain. That way the party could go on, rain or shine. As he said, they probably wouldn't need the covering.

A LITTLE HIKE

Ben dropped by the mill house on Sunday the 8th' to see how David and Jill were making out with their preparations. He could tell right away that they were rather frantic about minor details of the upcoming event.

"You two seem a little stressed out over this whole wedding thing. Why don't the three of us, or four, if I can talk Janet into it, take a little hike on Tuesday. I will talk to Janet about it when I pick her up at the airport tonight," Ben suggested. "David, you and Jill should see a bit more of the country around here. The trailhead for the hike I have planned is only a few miles from Leadville. I promise this hike will relieve your stress. It will be a day you will remember," Ben promised.

"Well Jill, do you think we can spare one day before everyone arrives to do something fun and exciting? I could use a break from work myself. What say you?" David asked.

"Sure, a nice hike would be a good idea. I am up for that."

"Swell, I will ask Janet tonight. The weather looks good, at least for the next few days, so what about Tuesday the 10th?" Ben suggested.

"Sounds great. Let's do it," David responded.

"A couple of things, I suppose you both have some good hiking boots. You will also probably want to bring a day pack with water bottles, jackets, sunglasses, and perhaps suntan lotion. I will pick up some sandwiches and you two bring some chips and sodas. You two can drive to my house in Leadville and we can take my truck to the trailhead. Try and get there by 7am," Ben requested.

"That early?" Jill exclaimed.

"Oh yes, we must get to a 'good mountaineers' start, you know."

Despite having to get up at a ridiculous early hour, David and Jill made it to Ben's house by a few minutes after 7 am. Dressed, with pop tarts in hand, they found Ben, and surprisingly, Janet, spry and chipper, ready to go.

"I see you guys appear to have your hiking boots and day packs. There seems to be one item of equipment missing though, hiking poles. Every Colorado hiker needs to be properly equipped. So, as my wedding present to you, Jill and David, here is a pair of new Leki hiking poles," Ben said as he presented them with poles.

"Thanks man, these are really a nice surprise," David responded as he and Jill gracefully accepted the gifts.

Soon they had Ben's Ford crew cab loaded and ready to head out. It was a brisk morning. Ben said it was forty-five degrees but that it might be cooler where they were going. The sun was just beginning to bring a golden glow of light to the snow on the high peaks that were some miles away.

"Ben, tell us a bit about where we will be hiking?" Jill asked.

"Well, Jill, I thought I would take 'you all' (isn't that what you southerners say?) to a little hill so you can get the lay of the land. It is only about a four-mile hike. Truthfully, it is a tad steep. We are going to Mt. Elbert."

"Say, I think I have heard about that peak," David commented, while Googling Mt. Elbert on his I-phone. "Oh shit! That is the highest mountain in Colorado! It's 14,440 feet tall. Are you kidding me?" David exclaimed.

At this point, Jill and Janet both gasped at the idea of such a thing. Ben tried his best to reassure them all the way to the trailhead. He told the Southerners that he had hiked to the top several times and was sure they could do it. It would be a slow steep trail, but no actual mountaineering skills were necessary.

It was 8:15 as they unloaded and placed their lunches and drinks in their day packs. The morning was still quite chilly at the trailhead, so everyone started out in jackets. Ben led the procession as they embarked on a well-worn trail leading upward. They soon left the few scrub spruce and larch trees behind and saw nothing but the rock of the monster peak looming over them.

"Will there be snow on top, assuming we are able to make it up there?" Janet asked.

"Should be."

"I bet it will be cold up there."

"Well, if there is snow, you can bet on it being pretty cool," Ben joked.

The marker at the start of the trail indicated that the summit was 4.3 miles. They soon discovered it was not the distance that made it so bad, it was the ever-increasing steepness of the trail, which climbed nearly four thousand feet in only four miles. They all soon found out just how out of shape they really were.

The brisk morning made the trek much more pleasant. It wasn't long before the exertion had all four shedding their jackets when they stopped to hydrate. A few clouds also kept the sun somewhat at bay. The higher they climbed, the more spectacular the distant view became. Another nicety of the hike was the absence of many other people. As the sun peaked out more and more, the group stopped to smear suntan lotion on exposed skin.

"I wonder where all the other hikers are? There were several cars at the trailhead," David commented.

"Probably passed out dead up ahead," Jill speculated.

"I hope they aren't all at our lunch spot," Ben commented.

"What lunch spot? And when do we get there? I am needing a rest stop," Janet panted.

"Not too much further up ahead. There are a lot of grand boulders and it's only about a thousand feet up to the summit from there," Ben said.

"What about a rest stop for other needs?" Jill asked.

"Oh yeah, guess you gals need a potty break. Out here

it's trees or rocks. Since we are above the tree line, you will just have to tinkle behind some large rock. I will give everyone a plastic bag for TP. You know we must pack it out."

"Well, that is good to know. Glad I did my constitutional before we left this morning," David commented, offering more information than was needed.

Finally, about eleven thirty, after numerous stops, the struggling foursome made it to Ben's boulders. The view was truly grand. Before them to the west were endless snow-covered peaks. The air was thin at their thirteen-thousand-foot altitude. Coupled with the chilly breeze made it quite brisk. The first thing they all did before lunch was to re-jacket. Ben's worries of a large group occupying his boulders was unfounded. There was only one other couple there. That couple was in a discussion about whether to turn back or press on.

As they broke out lunches, a similar conversation was occurring between Jill and Janet in Ben's group. Ben kept urging everyone on and upward by describing the even more spectacular view at the top, not to mention the glory of having mastered the tallest peak in Colorado. Ben had chosen well with his choice of hearty Italian sub sandwiches with everyone declaring them to really hit the spot.

Following a much-needed rest, hydration, and nourishment, the whole group agreed to try and reach the summit. In an effort to keep the gals interested and not to go at a pace too exhausting on them, Ben suggested that the gals take turns leading. Jill led off first. Soon after lunch, they started encountering spots of lingering snow where the trail was shaded by boulders. An hour later, they were only a few hundred feet from their goal. They stopped for candy bars and more water.

With the goal in site, the foursome was re-invigorated and launched into their final push for the summit. A new challenge was now added to the endeavor, that being they were now hiking through crusty snow patches. These required great caution and their tipped hiking poles were of great benefit.

It was 1:30 when they finally reached the large cairn atop Mt. Elbert. With a great yell, the group celebrated victory.

Jill announced, "I want to take pictures in all directions. Look you can see part of the trail far down below. I can't believe we made it. This is wonderful. David, do go back down the trail there so I can get your picture."

"Are you crazy? You want me to go down to take my picture, only to have me climb back up. I have a better idea. I will stay here hugging the cairn, you climb back down, and I can take a picture of you and the others below me."

The few clouds made the skyward view grand as well. To the North and West there were snowcapped peaks as far as the eye could see. All in all, it was a thrilling experience for all and something all agreed they would long remember. Too soon, Ben announced they should head back as they did not want to still be on the mountain when the sun went down. By the time they started their descent, complaints about sore feet commenced.

"Just ignore the pain. Everything will be ok. We will be down soon," was Ben's advice.

A cheerful, but exhausted foursome made it back to the

trailhead by 5:30. Tired, dirty, and with sore feet, they still elected to stop at the 'prime rib place' in Leadville before splitting up and David and Jill heading back to the Old Mill to collapse.

The next day, four days before the big day, Jill's parents arrived. They were to be staying at the Mill House in one of the upstairs bedrooms. The following day, David's folks were to arrive. They to, were to be staying at the Mill House.

Both sets of parents had visited the house before, though at separate times. This would be the first time they were all staying together. It was also the first time the house had been fully occupied.

It was the day of the rehearsal and dinner following. The plan was for the rehearsal to take place in a meeting room at the largest and nicest of the two hotels in downtown Leadville. This made logical sense since that was where a number of the participants would be staying.

After the brief rehearsal, the group would walk the two blocks from the hotel to Quincey's, where the dinner for the dozen would take place. Well, at least that was the plan. Things almost worked that way.

To start with, the minister got confused and arrived at the restaurant first. He called David and was quickly re-routed to the rehearsal location. Then Quincey's had set up for eight rather than twelve. Oh, and yes, Bill had started drinking a bit too early. But on the bright side Janet was very meek with no pranks played. Jill would later credit Ben with the miraculous change in Janet. Regrettably, Jill would not feel that way twenty-four hours later.

It was the night before the wedding and all through the house panic ensued. The weather that had been fine, appeared set to change and now, well it might not be fine. One forecast called for partly cloudy and mild, an hour later there was a chance of rain, and finally one forecaster even mentioned snow. No one in the wedding really expected snow on June 14th. This however was Colorado and at an elevation of ten thousand feet, it could snow most anytime.

And snow it did! David and Jill awoke the morning of their wedding to find it cloudy with the temperature a chilly forty degrees. Certainly not ideal for an outdoor wedding. The good news was according to the quite unreliable weather forecast, it was to be sunny and sixty degrees that afternoon. That forecast never came close.

David and Jill were determined to hold their ceremony as planned down by the Old Mill. They intended to do this despite sun, rain, or even snow. In the hour before the ceremony, while Jill was getting into her gown, snow it did.

David was quite excited, and yes nervous. The morning of the big event could not have started more different than that which the pair had long envisioned. Obviously, they never considered snow for an outdoor wedding in June. Then again there were other shocking things as well.

Jill's mother and her maid of honor, Janet, were helping Jill get dressed and ready. Looking back on it later, Jill would realize how odd it was for Janet to cut out from helping her early, saying she needed to change herself, when she already had her bridesmaid dress on. At the time, Jill just thought it was Janet being her inconsiderate self.

By the time the ceremony began, the decision had already been made to utilize the large tent rather than to have it out in the open down by the mill. They still planned on pictures there.

Using the tent still meant the guests and participants and guests would have to walk carefully and quickly through the falling snow from the house down to the tent. Some carried umbrellas but most, the younger crowd, relished the experience of a snowfall wedding. Getting a few snowflakes in their hair seemed ok.

After seating the guests and family, the groomsmen, decked out in their blue suits, took up their positions up front on the right of the minister. Following the groomsmen came the groom. The bride's attendants, all-in pale-yellow dresses, took their position opposite the minister. Then Janet, the Maid of Honor, entered. As David watched her enter, he turned to his best man, Bill and said, "Oh shit!"

It seemed as though Janet had jettisoned her pale-yellow bridesmaid dress and was now decked out in white, like the bride. David could vividly imagine Jill's reaction. He didn't have to wait long to confirm his suspicions, since with the start of the traditional wedding march, Jill and her father came forward through the snow. As she drew near, David could see her crimson face glowing through her veil. He knew her red face was from anger rather than the cold.

As Jill stood next to him in front of the minister, David tried his best to make subtle gestures to her to calm her. He was so afraid she might erupt during the ceremony. David had already formed a plan for revenge on Janet.

After the 'you may now kiss the bride,' David casually bent down in the snow and formed a snowball and motioned to Jill with his head toward Janet as he presented the snowball to his new wife. Jill promptly launched the snowball quite accurately into Janet's face.

Fearing this occurrence might instigate a snowball fight, David immediately spoke to the audience, "Say, before any more snowballing, how about we take a few pictures, change, and then we can really go at it." Jill tossed her bouquet away from Janet. As if by fate, a sudden gust of wind brought it into Janet's outstretched hands. David and Jill proceeded to wade through the snow down to the Old Mill for a series of snow filled wedding shots, much to the photographer's displeasure.

The plan had been for the first dance and the father and daughter dance to have taken place on the deck up at the house. With the deck now snow-covered, dancing had to be in the great room instead.

As promised, soon the wedding party had changed and were ready for snowballing, eating, and drinking.

The band had planned to setup in the tent after the ceremony, but then with the snow and cold, they moved into the great room instead. The elder crowd largely remained there while the younger ones took to drunken snow play.

By late that afternoon, the party goers were a bedraggled, drunk bunch. Some of the older folks even partook in the snowballing.

Cutting the cakes was the finishing touch for an otherwise crazy wedding in the snow.

As you can imagine, there were some very hard words

addressed to Janet from Jill and her parents. Ben, wisely, was mild in his defense of his girlfriend's inappropriate display.

There were wedding gifts galore. Of special note was the gift from Bill Brooks, Tim, and Ben. They had decided the young pair needed a hot tub to go out on their deck for those cool months. Other than the usual china and dishes, Bill gave the pair a nice hammock and Janet gave them a nice gas grill for the deck.

The last of family and guests left just as the sun was starting to set. Fortunately, by then the snow had stopped, leaving an accumulation of only a couple of inches. Also fortunate was the snow appeared not to be a problem for David and Jill to escape for their honeymoon the next morning. Both sets of parents were coming back over to the house the morning after to cleanup any remaining mess.

For their honeymoon, David and Jill had settled on a location far from both Georgia and Colorado. They had chosen Hawaii. For a grand wedding present, Jill's parents were paying for their honeymoon. With that in mind, they had decided to splurge and go to an exotic place neither had ever been. Their flight was out of Denver at 1 pm the following afternoon.

The pair departed for the airport at the early hour of 9:30 to allow plenty of time. Shortly after they had checked their bags, who do they see at the airport but Janet and Ben.

Rushing over to them, Jill said, "What are you two doing here?"

"Oh, didn't we tell you? We are going with you two on your honeymoon in Hawaii," Janet announced.

A now fully energized Jill piped up with, "Like hell you are!"

"Calm yourself, Sis; Ben and I are only going as far as San Fran. Going to spend a few days there taking in the sites. Ben said it is a place I should see."

"So, Ben, you have visited San Francisco before, I gather?" David asked.

"Sure, it is a terrific town. A little larger than Leadville," he said laughing.

"That's great. David, we probably need to check it out in the future, don't you think?" Jill commented.

With that the couples wished each other well on their adventures.

18. Life At The Old Mill

At the airport in Denver, David struggled to load all their luggage on a baggage cart. In addition to an assortment of souvenirs and gifts for others, they had a case of pineapples. Jill was concerned with promptly getting pineapples to Tim and his wife, as well as Ben and Janet.

"What do you say we go and meet our neighbors, the Baileys' and take them a pineapple?" Jill suggested.

"Yah, I want to keep a few of these pineapples for us. I am really going to miss all that tasty fruit we had there," David said.

"Hawaii was wonderful, but I am glad to be back to our new home," Jill said as they drove back to the Old Mill from Denver that afternoon.

"I agree, Home Sweet Home, or should I say, Mill Sweet Mill."

"Perhaps we can get a couple of our best Hawaii photos made as large prints and framed to help decorate a couple of bare walls. What do you think?" Jill asked.

"Great idea, we both like variety in things and I feel we have some really great photos, such as that dinner cruise one."

To their great relief, the house seemed in fine order. It appeared as though their families had done a good job of clean-up following the wedding reception and their honeymoon departure. The only thing out of place was the book that apparently Janet had left on their bed, entitled "Getting Pregnant."

"Looks like your sister has been here and has plans for us."

"Well, she might just be on to something this time. What do you think? She may be, but you and I need to decide that. We don't need any pushing by Janet or our families, do we?" Jill said.

"No, you are right. By the way, can you see Janet with a new-born?"

"Perhaps that's just what she needs, though she probably needs a good husband first," Jill added.

"Do you think she might find one in Ben?"

"Don't know, but you may be right. I do like him a lot. He has been a stabilizing force for her, in spite of him having some reckless habits. He is a good guy. Almost as good as the one I got," Jill said.

"Go on, I love your complements, though I don't think I did so bad with my choice of a mate either," he admitted.

A couple of days after they returned, right before July 4th, Tim stopped by to see the newlyweds. He said that he wanted to make sure everything at the house was ok. Tim asked them if they were really going to spend the winter at the Old Mill? They told him they were. At that he offered a raft of suggestions on what they should consider doing to prepare for winter.

One suggestion Tim made was for David and Jill to introduce themselves to the couple living just outside their gate who they had yet to meet. Tim said that couple had been there five years and he thought they would be a big asset to them. He said their last name was Baily.

"David, Jill told me you have a degree in Construction Management. I also understand you are planning to live here fulltime, is that right?" Tim inquired.

"That's correct," David responded. "Jill has lined up a teaching job in Leadville, and I hope to try and find work there as well."

Tim said, "I thought that might be the case. There is an opportunity you just might be interested in. As you know, for the last five years, in addition to looking after the mill property, I have been managing work for a local contractor in Leadville."

Tim continued, "The name of the firm is 'Timberstone Builders'. The owner is in his late sixties. He is thinking about trying to sell the business. He has offered it to me if I want to buy it. You know I am sixty myself and at my age I think it would be foolish to undertake such a venture by myself.

"So far, I haven't been able to get Ben too interested, though hopefully that may change. If you would be interested in coming in with me, we could buy the business. I could stay and get you started, then you could buy me out, or you and Ben could have your own construction company. Do you think that might be something that you would consider?"

"Absolutely. I would like to know more about the company and the work it has done. Of course, the financials would be important, but, yes, that does sound interesting," David said.

With that conversation, David started to take a hard look at the 'Timberstone Builders' prospect with Tim. David and Jill had already discovered that Tim and his wife knew a lot of people in the area and had proven a great resource. He felt the venture would be an excellent way to break into a business in the area in his chosen field of work.

That Saturday, David and Jill took one of their pineapples and followed Tim's suggestion and walked down the road to introduce themselves to the Baileys. Their neighbors thanked them for the Hawaiian treat. They found the middle-aged couple, Nancy and Daniel, to be very friendly. It seemed that Nancy was also a school teacher. Nancy said that perhaps they could ride into Leadville together for their classes. This sounded grand to Jill.

Daniel was also quite nice. He had been some sort of an investment adviser for a large bank in Denver, but he had retired early. They built their house and moved there five years earlier. He was now a writer of fiction and had two books published.

After telling the couple their paintings story, Daniel and Nancy both appeared quite astonished. Daniel said their story would make for a great book. He offered to help them make that happen. Nancy, meanwhile, told them that she and Daniel had two children about their ages.

Their son Sam graduated from the University of Colorado about a year earlier with a degree in Geology. Presently he was working for a mining concern in Wyoming.

Their daughter, Kate, was a senior at the university study-ing Business Management. They went on to say that, Kate was spending a month in Germany and due back home the first week in August. Nancy said she hoped Jill and David could meet her when she returned.

As Tim had promised, the Baileys shared a great deal of information with the newlywed's, in particular what to expect in wintering there. David and Jill invited Nancy and Daniel to have dinner with them at the Old Mill the fol-lowing Saturday evening.

"They sure seemed like a nice couple, and what a co-incidence she is also a school teacher. I must talk to her more about that when they are over next Saturday," Jill commented.

"Yes, I agree. They will be handy and good company this winter I believe. Did you pick up on their son being a geologist. I would sure like to get him to look at our gold mine and advise us if it is worth messing with."

When the Baileys were over for dinner, Jill mentioned that she and David were considering getting a dog. With that, Nancy asked if they would consider a golden retriever puppy. Jill responded she felt they would. David nodded his ok with that. Nancy then told them she knew a couple that had golden puppies eight weeks ago and they were going to be trying to sell them soon. David and Jill made plans to look at them.

The following weekend, the pair made an appointment to look at the golden puppies. They were immediately taken by one of the frisky pups with a unique white marking on its otherwise standard golden fur coat. The couple selling the puppies said they should be weaned, dewormed, and ready to pick up in about ten days. David and Jill anxiously awaited the puppy sellers call so they could get the dog.

A week later the call came. David and Jill had already decided on a name for their new addition. She was to be named Millie, a name that they felt matched their new home. Having a rambunctious puppy around was definitely a learning experience for the pair. Shoes had to be put up high. Then there was the house training. Jill had already read up on just how that was supposed to be done. Unfortunately, they found it not to be so simple. Fortunately, they had a lot of patience.

It was a month later. David was at Tim's house reviewing the numbers for the Timberstone deal and preparing an offer for the company when Tim enlightened David about his son Ben. He told David that he was pretty sure Ben was going to propose to Janet the following week. He said Ben was planning to fly to Virginia where Janet was finishing her final semester of school.

"Well, that is news, I hope it works out. I believe it will be a good match for both," David said.

Tim commented, "I agree and I am pretty excited."

David couldn't wait to report the news about Ben and Janet to Jill.

"Say Jill, my meeting with Tim about buying 'Timberstone' went well and it appears we are going to offer to buy it. That is not the news, however. It seems that Ben is flying to Virginia next week to propose to Janet."

"No! really? That is amazing. She will be shocked."

"Do you think she will accept?"

"Of course, I believe she really loves him. Marriage, I feel, will settle them both down. Have you not noticed how much they both have changed since they have been dating? I can't wait," Jill said. "Then again, my parents may have to move to Colorado," she added.

Sure enough, a week later Jill got the call from Janet announcing she was in fact engaged to Ben and they were to be married at Christmas in Atlanta.

"Well, David, you were right. My sis is engaged to Ben. They are planning a rather quick December wedding in Atlanta after she graduates from Virginia the first of December. You don't reckon she is pregnant, do you?" Jill asked.

"You never know, could be. With your sister, she might be."

A month later, Tim and David became the new owners of Timberstone Builders, LLC.

In addition to tying up about one hundred thousand of their funds in the 'Timberstone Builders,' the deal was to turn out to be quite a labor-intensive venture. The company had a total of six projects underway, including a couple of million-dollar homes, a shopping center, an office building, and a school.

If all these projects turned out well, the partners would recoup most of their investment within a year. Their biggest concern was precuring future work. David felt ill-equipped since he had not yet established many business contacts. Initially this burden would fall to Tim, though David committed to helping.

Back at the Old Mill, there was still plenty of work going on there as well. David was renovating and upgrading Tim's old cabin into a comfortable guest cottage for when they had an abundance of company. Of course, Millie was there trying to help out by carrying away the wood scraps.

Then there was the Old Mill itself. Though he had it generating limited power, David and Jill also decided to add solar panels. They chose a location where they could catch the sun but not be obtrusive.

Tim told David one thing about the mill that David had failed to consider. It would have to be shut down in winter. Apparently, according to Tim, Mill Creek would freeze solid during the winter. In addition, the ice would damage the millwheel if it was left engaged. The thought of their large wild stream freezing came as somewhat of a shock to David and Jill. That was only the first of several warnings of what to expect for their life there during the long winter.

As the middle of August rolled around, David was extremely busy with Tim and their new company. David quickly learned that every minute during the summer season was vital for construction with the climate in the mountains of Colorado. Apparently, due to snow and the cold, nearly all outdoor and a great lot of interior work shuts down from the first of November until the end of March.

This climate restriction required Tim and David to work at a furious pace to complete the two houses and the exterior work on the other four projects by November first. They agreed it was doable. The completion fee they were to receive would go a long way toward carrying the young company through the winter.

David, on the other hand, was acutely aware of his responsibility to spend time with his new wife. Several people had cautioned him about how important it was to do that. Another growing concern David had was how prepared they were for the winter. Based on some research and the local folks he had talked to, he learned that due to their high elevation, it could often get below zero and a twelve-inch snow seemed to be quite common. He was looking forward to snow, but from what he was learning, it made him a little frightful.

The first of the million-dollar homes was for a doctor and his wife. Doctor Frank Shafer and his wife Julie were really a great couple whom David had quickly bonded with. The Shafer's were very pleased with the house and most anxious for it to be complete. It seemed that they were planning a big house warming party before the holidays.

Dr. Shafer was the Chief Administrator of the local hospital and as such knew about everyone in town. He invited Tim and his wife as well as David and Jill to his grand house- warming party set for Saturday, October 29th. That was assuming Tim and David had it completed by October 1st so they could have it furnished by then. Both firmly committed to doing so.

Both Jill and David were really looking forward to the big event. It would be their first big chance to be introduced to the elite of Leadville. Mr. Shafer said his wife had invited about one hundred to the party. Like any woman, Jill was fixated on what to wear. David, not so much. He just planned to wear a coat and tie.

The couple didn't have to wait too long for the first snow of the season. On September 12th there was a beautiful wet four inches that coated everything. It did, however, present Jill with what was to be an ongoing challenge, that being getting into Leadville for her school class. In this case, David drove Jill in in his four wheeled drive SUV. That snow was just the first of many that would greatly restrict the pair over the long winter.

That snow set David scrambling to complete plans for their wintering at the Old Mill. He had to finish laying up more firewood. He had acquired a chain saw and was becoming proficient with it as well as splitting firewood. David had also installed a gas fired home generator and stocked up on propane should they need it. One thing Tim suggested was that he keep the company's Bobcat front end loader at the Old Mill for the winter. He could use it to plow out his driveway. Tim brought it out and showed David how to use it.

The Schafer party was a really big event for the small town of Leadville. It was a who's who of the elite permanent residents of the relatively small community. Tim already knew many of the invitees, but for David and Jill, it was their first real introduction.

That party, and the glowing complements the Schafer's laid on Tim and David's 'Timberstone Company' was soon to pay off with contracts for two more large homes to start in the spring. So, by the first of November, the future looked bright.

Plans were made for David and Jill to fly to Atlanta for two weeks during Christmas and to attend Janet's wedding. Tim and David agreed to shut down Timberstone and give their workers those two weeks off. Tim and his wife, as well as a few of their friends, were going to Atlanta for Ben's wedding. Quite fortunately, the Baileys had graciously offered to keep their, now house trained, Millie, while they were away.

It had been over six months since the pair had been back to their home town of Atlanta. They were really looking forward to seeing friends and family, and yes getting back to some warmer weather and away from what was becoming too much snow.

Ben and Janet's wedding was a more typical wedding than Jill's and David's had been. No snow at their Atlanta wedding on December 27th. Theirs was held in Jill's parents' church with their minister presiding. There were two attendants and Jill was maid of honor. She did not wear white to match the bride. David was Ben's best man and two of Ben's friends from Colorado were there as groomsmen. All in all, it was a really nice affair, without the drama that had occurred at Jill and David's wedding.

Atlanta, the wedding, and Christmas had been fun, but getting back home was a welcome thing as well. On the drive back from the airport, the pair discussed New Year's resolutions. Jill asked David if he had any?

David responded, "Yes, I think one resolution we should make is to move forward with giving to others. You know when we inherited all that money, we discussed doing that. So far, we haven't done too much of that. I got a lot of pleasure from helping the family of your student whose house had burned. I want to give more to others. I think we should set a goal to give away at least five percent of what we have each year. Especially since we are making more than that much from our investments."

"David, I wholeheartedly agree with that. You are right, we have so much and there are so many in need. Let's do make that a resolution this new year. I have one additional resolution. Again, this is something we have discussed but so far have failed to do. I want us to find a church we are both comfortable with and start attending church regularly."

"Yes, you are right, I certainly agree. Actually, that sort of ties into giving, don't you think?" He asked.

"It does. As always it seems we are thinking alike, my soulmate."

Upon their return, they quickly encountered what they were to face for the next four months. Mill Creek Road had not been properly plowed. Beyond that, their driveway now had an accumulation of a foot of snow and their front porch and rear deck had almost that much.

David frantically set about clearing the drive and the road with the Bobcat. He quickly mastered the machine and appeared to be having so much fun with it Jill wanted to try it out. Then he and Jill together shoveled off the decks, finishing just before another snow immediately followed, dumping another six inches. The winter was to follow with this digging out exercise repeating itself many times.

Occasionally they would get together with the Baileys, taking turns having each other over for dinner and to watch a movie DVD. Nancy would often give Jill a ride in to school, a gesture she really appreciated.

By winter's end, David and Jill were beginning to question whether being snowbound all winter was really what they were cut out for.

19. The Gold Mine & Another Painting

Following David and Jill's return to the Old Mill after the wedding and Christmas, they had been playing catch-up. First with Millie. Their rambunctious pup was more than excited to see her masters again. David and Jill were glad to have their fur baby back home. The pair profusely thanked the Baileys for keeping her.

Jill's teaching had resumed and David's job now focused on finishing all the interior work on their ongoing projects. As to the weather, it was snow and cold. By the time they got back to the Old Mill, as Tim had predicted, Mill Creek had completely frozen and failed to flow.

After returning from their honeymoon, Ben and Janet settled into life in Leadville. Ben was going to start working as a manager for Timberstone. David was quite pleased with this as he hoped that would allow him a bit more free time to spend at the Old Mill and with Jill. Janet was staying busy preparing advertising and flyers for local establishments, as well as doing some song writing.

David's job particularly kept him tied up most of the

time every week. Jill was looking forward to having the next summer off from teaching school. As a result of these commitments, the pair had very little time to think about the gold mine, let alone time to spend exploring the old mine.

While having dinner with the Baileys in April, they learned that their son Sam was coming for a visit the 1st of May. With that news, David and Jill felt they should have him inspect their mine. Also, by then the snows of winter were finally dwindling away. The world of snow was leaving the Old Mill. With the arrival of spring in the Rockies, David and Jill were energized. They were well along in making an abundance of plans. Jill's school would be out in a month, just as David would be getting busy with Timberstone's new projects.

While they were discussing their summer plans, the gold mine was a prime topic.

The pair had expressed some thoughts to each other initially about trying to mine it, or perhaps open it to tours. Having never actually explored the mine, exploring it climbed to the top of their list. This was particularly true now with Sam, the geologist, pending arrival.

"Jill, I asked Tim yesterday what the condition of the mine was. Surprisingly, he said he couldn't say as he had never been in it. Apparently, Bill never gave him a key to the gate at the mine entrance. As far as he knew, no one had been in there since Henry died."

"That is a bit strange. I would have thought Tim would have been all through it. Makes me wonder if there is something lurking in there we might want to see."

"My thoughts exactly. What say we check it out the next pretty weekend? I will get us a couple of good flashlights," David said.

"Sounds like a plan."

"Jill, have you by chance seen the key Bill gave us for the lock on the gate at the mine entry? I seem to have misplaced it."

"No, I have no idea where it might be."

David bemoaned, "Guess I will have to call Bill and see if by chance he happens to have another."

"According to Bill, Henry left him two keys to the mine gate lock, saying they were the only two. Bill went on to say he had never been in the mine. He commented that Henry was always rather secretive about it. Bill volunteered to mail me the other key tomorrow after he has a copy made, just in case the second one gets lost in the mail."

An hour after David had spoken to Bill, he called back saying, "On second thought, why don't I just bring you the key on Saturday? I had meant to give you two a house warming present and failed to bring it to the wedding. If you don't have plans, why don't you show off your grilling skills on that new grill and cook some burgers for my wife and me?. Is that, ok?" Bill asked.

"Absolutely, look forward to it," David responded.

"Jill, Bill Brooks is going to bring us a key to the mine on Saturday along with a house warming gift. Wants us to crank up the grill for lunch with he and his wife. What do you think about that?"

"Sounds great. Will be good to see them again. I wonder what sort of house warming gift he might bring?" Jill commented. "I will pick up some things for our lunch with them on my way back from school on Friday."

It was the first Saturday in May when Bill and his wife Lane showed up late morning at the Old Mill. David and Jill greeted them and ushered them out to the porch. It was a rather brisk mountain morning and all had their jackets on. David had already turned on the radiant heater tower for everyone to congregate under.

As they sat down, Bill handed David the key and said, "Here is the other mine gate key. In the file with that key was this smaller key as well. I have no idea what it goes to. Perhaps you will find out. I am glad to see you two survived your first mountain winter," Bill said.

"You know, it really wasn't too bad, though it is a good thing we both enjoy snow, because we sure had a plenty!" Jill said, while hoping she didn't grow a Pinocchio nose.

"We were completely snowbound for only a week though. My four-wheel drive and snow tires sure paid off," David announced proudly.

Lane spoke up saying, "Bill, before you forget it, go to the car and get the gift we brought for them."

"Good thinking, dear. Be right back." Soon Bill reappeared carrying a rather large, flat object in a black plastic bag.

"As I recalled, this old house had a lot of vacant wall space. We felt you might need a bit more artwork to decorate your log walls with. You know I have several of your uncle's paintings and thought you could use another one, besides those of the Old Mill. By the way, where are you going for your anniversary? Perhaps this will give you some ideas," Bill commented.

Jill took off the wrapping and they discovered a beautiful seascape painting by Henry Mack. The painting featured dunes, surf, and a beautiful white sandy beach stretching into the distance. There was an absence of people in the painting, that was other than two blond headed young children. There appeared to be a slightly older little boy and a little girl building a sandcastle.

As Jill held the painting for David to see, she suddenly shouted, "There is another note on the back." Laying the painting face down on the table for all to see, she read aloud the note, "You are where I am."

"Not another note! What can this note possibly mean? Do you think there could be another painting out there with the rest of this note on it?" David asked. "Where is the scene in the painting? Bill, what do you know about this?"

Bill said, "Yes, I had seen the note when Henry gave this painting to me. I asked him about it. At first, he didn't answer, then he said, 'Well just imagine yourself as though you were taking a picture.' That was all he ever said. He never said where he painted it."

"I suspect without any other information, it will be difficult to ever find the location," David commented.

Never the quitter, Jill piped up, "Well we found this place didn't we!"

The foursome had a great visit. Jill showed off the decorating she had done to the house since the wedding. Then they all looked around the house for the perfect place to hang the seascape of Henry's. The group finally chose a location on one of the great room walls. Following a delicious grilled lunch, Bill and Lane bid David and Jill farewell.

After the couple had departed, David and Jill discussed their new painting. They wondered if this could be the same seascape painting the Flanders said that Henry told them about. They remembered them saying he was doing such a painting when he last spoke to them. Perhaps they held the key to the scene's location. But again, Bill Brooks had it, perhaps he knew more about it.

It appeared that they had another location to find. Another curiosity for them, who were the children in the painting. After all, the Flanders had said Henry painted it on a deserted beach.

Jill spoke up, offering a shocking possibility, "Do you think they could be our kids?"

"Wow, you don't really think so, do you? That would just be too much. Guess time will tell," David responded.

"The boy looks older, maybe six and the girl about four, don't you think? If that is the case, we better get to looking for the place. And also, we better get busy, if you know what I mean." She smiled and laughed.

"Yah, I hear you. I have been thinking about us having kids as well." Then David added, "And I will have so much fun, getting you that way."

The very next day, on Sunday, the pair decided to explore their gold mine. Now with Bill's key, that was possible. With the key and flashlights in hand, the pair was more than ready.

"How dangerous do you think it will be going into the

mine? Could there be snakes or even bats or a wild animal in there?" Jill asked.

He replied, "I don't know. We will have to go slow and really watch our steps."

As they hiked up the slope of old mine tailings, they noticed an old rusty wheeled mine cart. There were also scraps of metal and wood timbers littering the slope. Soon they stood at the old rusty metal gate. Looking through the gate, sunlight illuminated only a short distance into the seemingly horizontal shaft. They saw what appeared to be railroad rails leading into the dark.

Based on the difficulty getting the padlock unlocked, it was apparent that the gate had not been opened in a long time.

Finally, the lock was off. As David slowly opened the gate, the rusted hinges gave off a slightly scary sound that echoed from the dark cavern. The beams from their flash-lights penetrated the darkness of the six-foot wide seven-foot-high rough tunnel carved into the rock of the mountain. David let out a shout, thinking it might scare out any wild animal that might reside within. His sudden shout caused Jill to jump and to use a bit of foul language on him for scaring her.

When nary a beast emerged, the pair entered the tunnel. They found the walls to be rough jagged rock. Every ten or twelve feet, there were old deteriorating timbers that appeared to have been placed there to support the rock tunnel roof above. Carefully the two inched their way forward.

Soon they came to a wider section where another tunnel

branched off to their right. Right past this junction, they encountered an assortment of old metal objects. They appeared to be old mining implements, last used years earlier. Shining the light on the pile, David noticed what appeared to be a small black tool box. What really piqued his interest was that it had a reasonably modern, small padlock on it.

Besides the old box, there was a series of numbers stenciled on the rough tunnel walls. The numbers, in white paint, made no sense to either of them. David pulled out his I-phone and took a picture of the numbers painted on the wall.

"Jill, look at what I have found. Why do you think this old box has a lock on it? See, the lock looks newer than the box. I believe I will take this back to the house and try and get the lock off."

The side tunnel soon ended. They had been continuously inspecting the tunnel walls for any sign of gold or white quartz, which they had learned was frequently found with gold. Having found none in that tunnel, they made their way back to the main tunnel. Once there, they again followed the two iron rails deeper into the dark.

Then ahead there was a speck of light and they felt the semblance of a breeze. They had come to another smaller shaft leading upward at a steep angle. Looking up, they could see it was partially blocked with debris. Clearly it led to the surface. David told Jill that it probably was a ventilation shaft. About fifty feet beyond the ventilation shaft, the rails ended, as did the tunnel.

With no obvious veins of gold having been discovered, the pair picked up the old locked box. After closing and relocking the gate, they headed back down toward the Old Mill carrying the metal box.

Jill commented, "At least there weren't any snakes or bats in there."

"Yah, but I didn't see any nut sized nuggets in there either. I fear our gold mine may be just a hole in the mountainside," David said. "Perhaps Sam can enlighten us a bit more about the prospects for the mine when he is here in a couple of days."

"Maybe I can get the lock off the box," David said contemplating how he might remove the lock.

As David struggled with the lock, trying to figure what tool he might use to get the lock off, Jill piped up, "What about that other key Bill brought. Do you think it might be for that lock?"

"Good idea, though I doubt it can be that simple," he responded.

Turned out it was just that simple. It was the key for the lock and soon the lock was off and the contents revealed. The box contained a few old tools, which appeared to belong there. Additionally, there were a few artists paint brushes, a single dried rose, two pea sized gold nuggets, and an envelope. After fingering the nuggets, David prepared to rip into the envelope. Jill suggested using a letter opener she took from the nearby rolltop desk.

Jill opened the envelope in a gentler fashion. The first item was a picture of a woman. Jill said, "You know I believe I have seen her picture before."

"That's odd," David commented. "You don't know who she is?"

"No, but …yes! I think this may be my great Aunt Carolyn, you know Henry's fiancé," she responded.

"Well, what with the artist brushes and all, this box clearly must have belonged to Henry, so the picture could very well be your Aunt Carolyn."

There also was a cryptic note with a series of numbers at the end. The note read: Oh, but the dreams I had. Now for young love to have and to the children never enjoyed. Only the beauty of untouched nature's glory. Share it as I have and I will live on in your doing it. Continue my chase and reap nature's beauty. In time, you may find another painting of mine. The note was signed H.M.M.

"Oh my! Another mystery. Do you think he is referring to the Seascape?" Jill asked.

"Could be. You know it may just be, what with this note, they might just be our children in the painting, and we are looking at that scene in real life. I am beginning to believe anything is possible when it comes to Henry with you and me," David said.

The next day, Jill rode to school with Nancy. Nancy invited Jill and David to have dinner Tuesday night with her, Daniel, and their son Sam. Their son was arriving that afternoon. Jill graciously accepted her invitation. The dinner was at 7:30. David had picked up some wine to take with them.

Sam was a handsome young man, maybe two years older than Jill and David. Jill started off the conversation by asking Sam about his job. His response caused her to regret having asked that question. It seemed he was rather unhappy where he was. Sam mentioned he was thinking of looking for another job back in Colorado, maybe even in a slightly different line of work. He even mentioned construction.

When Sam mentioned construction, David's ears perked up and his wheels of thought kicked in.

"Say, Sam, your parents may have told you already, but you see we happen to have an old gold mine on our property. It has long been abandoned. Probably it is not worth mining, but we would sure like it if you might have the time to look at it and give us your thoughts about it."

"Sure, I would be happy to look at it. Would tomorrow afternoon be, ok?"

"Yes, that will be great. How about 3:30?" David suggested.

"That is fine, I will meet you at your house then."

Nancy and Jill were back from school and enjoying a glass of wine out on the back deck when a slightly grubby David and Sam arrived back from the mine.

"So, you two dirty miners, what's the verdict, is there any gold in our mine?" Jill asked.

Sam responded, "Hard to say. I didn't see any promising veins, but there is a bit of quartz. If it were me, I probably wouldn't invest a lot in trying to expand the mine. Sorry not to give you better news. There are probably some 'wildcatters' out there who would have a go at it though."

"Well, thanks anyway. At least now we know not to count on vast wealth from our old mine," Jill said. "Come and have some wine, you two miners."

That night, with the information about the mine as a stimulant, David and Jill had a long conversation about their future. The winter had been quite tough on the couple.

David led off the conversation, "You know, Jill, I do so love this place and it has taken us so long to find it, but this last winter, I felt a bit smothered here. How about you, dear?"

"I completely agree. The first snow or two were great, so beautiful, but then it just kept snowing and all the snow just made it tough. Not being able to get out and do things. I didn't like that. I can see older couples such as Nancy and Daniel, or even Carolyn and Henry holding up here for the winter every year, but I mean, we are young. I want us to have children, and soon, but I would be terrified to be pregnant here in the winter," Jill added.

"Well, then, it is decided. We shall no longer stay isolated here all winter. Let me tell you something I have been thinking." David continued, "What if before next winter we find us a nice small house in Denver. I am sure you could get a teaching job there and I could find a job there as well.

"The one problem we would have is my involvement with Tim and Timberstone Builders. There may just be a solution to that as well. The other night at dinner with Sam, when he made that comment about his job dissatisfaction and that he might consider construction, it got me thinking. What if he came to work for Timberstone. I could sell him half my interest so he would have a strong incentive to make a success of it.

"Then there is Ben and Janet. Assuming Ben is going to come into the business and take over from Tim, the two of the 'young ins' could run the business in a year or two. We as 25% owners could still reap some of the benefits. To pull that off, I would need to stay somewhat involved until Ben and Sam got familiar with running the business. Of course, I would have to get Tim to agree with all this, but I believe he would. So, what do you think partner?" David asked.

Jill said, "It sounds like a great plan; however, it contains a lot of 'ifs.' But knowing you, or I should say we, I think it is doable. I am on board."

"Great, first I will talk to Tim tomorrow and if he is ok, I will then approach Sam with the offer."

And so, the couple set about an ambitious plan to shape their future. David explained his thoughts and the plan to Tim. As he had expected, Tim was very understanding and supportive of the whole thing. He was excited that Ben seemed to be getting interested in the business. David didn't say it, but his main concern was whether Janet could adjust to Leadville life.

With Tim's blessing, David went to meet with Sam.

"Sam, I have done a bit of thinking since we had dinner a few nights ago. You made a comment about being unhappy in your current line of work and you mentioned construction as a possibility. Is that still something you might consider?"

"Sure, do you know of a job?" Sam asked.

"I just might, assuming you are willing to start at the top," David said with a laugh.

"No, really, this is what I would like for you to consider. Jill and I are going to be starting a family soon and we are not going to be staying here all winter again. We are going to be moving to Denver. As you know, Tim and I own Timberstone Builders. I am committed to Tim to stay involved with the company as long as needed. Tim has his son, Ben. He is starting to learn the ropes to take over for him. What I propose is, to offer you the opportunity to acquire half my ownership in the company. Later if you are interested, perhaps I will sell you all my interest in it."

"I can't believe you would do that for me," Sam said.

"It is not a gift; you will have to work at it. You will have to hit the ground running. We are starting into our really busy season. I will be there to help you, but in the long term, I believe you and Ben can be great partners and can turn our little company into an even bigger success than it presently is now."

"Let's do it. When do I start?" Sam asked.

"Tomorrow!" David replied. "I will take you in to the office to meet Tim and Ben, then I will draw up a sales agreement between you and me."

With phase one of their plan in place, David and Jill moved forward with phase two. This involved weekend house hunting in Denver as well as Jill attempting to line up a teaching assignment for the Fall. David held off on seeking a job due to his continued involvement with Timberstone and the two rookie recruits. He expected to be making numerous trips back to Leadville. On the negative side, he expected that he would likely spend a number of lonely nights at the Old Mill house without Jill.

By mid-August, Jill had lined up a teaching position in a school located on the southern part of Denver. The pair had been fortunate to have located a great little house there near her school. They had put in a successful offer on it. It was a three bedroom two and a half bath, newer home located in a kid friendly subdivision with a great mountain view.

They moved in the week Jill began classes, though she had already been in Denver for nearly two weeks staying in a hotel while participating in a school training program. David had already made a number of what was to become numerous trips back and forth to Leadville.

After two months on the job, Sam was making good progress and was ready to take on managing projects on his own. With Ben having achieved a similar capability, Tim and David felt comfortable as they entered the slower fall and winter season.

Even better, the projects from the previous year had been completed. In addition to the two houses they picked up from the Schafer party contacts, they had acquired contracts to build two more nice homes, a restaurant, and a motel. David had recouped more than half the money he initially put into the venture.

The couple had let Sam have the renovated cabin at the Old Mill to use free of charge, but retained the Old Mill house for their frequent usage. Sam was also given a key to the mine as he wanted to do a bit more exploration in it. Having someone living on the property helped ease David and Jills minds when they were both in Denver. That fall and early winter, David was going back and forth, splitting his time between Leadville and Denver.

One new subject that David was becoming quite interested in was investments. David was destined to spend numerous nights that fall alone at the Old Mill. Jill had to remain in Denver due to her teaching. Frequently, Nancy and Daniel would invite him to have dinner with them. During these occasions, David had asked Daniel to teach him a bit about investing. He seemed like a good one to teach him since that was what he had been doing for the bank where he had worked in Denver.

David took it all in. With his new found knowledge, he and Jill began making some conservative investments in stocks and bonds. By years end, these investments were already showing promise with dividends and increases in valuation. For David and Jill, this proved exciting, though they remained mindful to remain cautious.

20. City Life & A New Arrival

As David and Jill began to settle into Denver lifestyle, they found more time to themselves in a more normal young adult life. Denver had much to offer and they had an international airport only forty-five minutes away. Now travel was way easier than from Leadville. Jill's school was larger and she had more opportunity to work with a wide variety of students. Though adjusting to her new school was a bit difficult at first, she soon really loved it, making many new friends with the faculty and with student's parents.

Millie adjusted quickly to suburban life. One of David's first projects at their new house was to build a four-foot-high picket fence around the back yard so Millie could roam free there when he and Jill were away during the day. In the evenings, the pair enjoyed walking her around the neighborhood, meeting other dogs and their owners.

One of their first free weekends in Denver, David and Jill visited the Denver Museum of Art to see the Henry Mack paintings on display there. The museum had seven of Henry's works on display. They were a bit disappointed there were not more, but having learned about his numerous private clients, they understood. Their favorite was a prairie scene complete with sagebrush and prairie dogs. They considered loaning or donating one of Henry's Old Mill paintings to the museum's collection but decided to hold on to both for the time being.

The pair were anxious to immerse themselves in to the young adult lifestyle. Joining a church seemed a good starting point. Jill and David discussed the pros and cons of their two faiths, her having been raised Baptist and he Methodist. It was a somewhat difficult decision. They finally agreed they both shared the same beliefs so it really didn't matter so much. After visiting one local Baptist Church and a Methodist they settled on Methodist. It was closer and appeared to have a surprisingly large attendance of young people their age.

Once they joined, they immediately became active in church activities. Jill decided to join the choir. David discovered that the church was sponsoring a Habitat for Humanity build. He promptly signed up to participate in the build. David learned that the church tried to do at least one build a year. Though this was his first time participating with Habitat, he really enjoyed putting his building experience to work helping a good cause. In this process, he made friends with several new dads.

With the new friends they were now making, Jill at her school and the pair at church, they started entertaining their new friends and neighbors. Frequently they were invited to attend functions and parties as well.

Now settled comfortably in their Denver home, the

couple decided that in addition to their dog, Millie, it was time to add another two-legged addition to their family. They were more than ready for kids, or so they thought.

The past years teaching and working with young children had led Jill to talk about how much she wanted a family. Though David had not experienced Jill's interaction with the cute little terrors, he agreed it was time.

It was right before they flew back to Georgia for Thanksgiving that Jill took her first pregnancy test. She decided not to tell anyone the result until after the Thanksgiving trip. That included David. It would be difficult but she wanted David and her to celebrate the event before their families started making plans for them over Thanksgiving. In addition, she wanted to be sure before she made an announcement.

David, not being entirely unaware of Jill's moods, sensed something was afoot. She seemed much more cheerful than he had seen her. It wasn't but a few days that her exuberance and her excitement led to his figuring it all out. She excitedly confirmed to him she was pregnant. The two were beside themselves with happiness. They did, however, agree that as Jill had planned, they would not mention their news when home for Thanksgiving. Jill was a bit concerned that her passing up wine might give them away. Her plan, should anyone comment about it, she would say it was to avoid complication with a medication she was taking.

Once again it was good to be around their families and briefly in a more moderate climate.

"So, you 'kids' ready to move back home yet?" Jill's mother asked just as she always did.

"You know it is mighty lonely here now without either you or Janet."

"No mom, we love the mountains out West. We will just have to visit often. You know you are always welcome at our homes," Jill commented. She was proud to imply they had two homes now.

Her mom called her out on that, saying, "I can't get use to my twenty-two-year-old daughter, just married, and already having two homes. You two need some kids!"

"We miss you and would like some grandkids. Your dad and I will have to just fly to Colorado now that you and Janet are both there. At least we can see both of you in a single trip."

David also felt bad for his parents and encouraged them to visit them often as well.

As was usually the case, they stuffed themselves with turkey and all the trimmings. Other news they picked up while home included that Bill and Beth had become engaged. David and Jill promised to try and make their wedding in May. They knew that was unlikely though, due to Jill's pregnancy.

"Boy, are they all going to be shocked Christmas when we break our news about our pregnancy," Jill commented on the plane ride back to Colorado.

"Yep, I expect they will. I can just hear our parents now begging us to move back to Georgia so they can be with their grandchild. In a way, I do feel sorry about that. You know it will also be more difficult on us not having them around to babysit and all. One thing I have thought of though is possibly spending the summer at the Old Mill house and having family come and visit us there. What do you think about that, Jill?" David asked.

"Sounds like a pretty good option. I know there will be lots of pressure to have us move back to Georgia, but we have made a life for ourselves and our family in a place we love."

"I agree completely. Perhaps we will need to buy a plane," he joked.

"No way are we going to blow money on an airplane."

"I hope Millie is ok. I hated to leave her with the dog sitter for a week but we had no choice," she said.

"Well, if we had a plane, she could have flown with us."

"And, if out gold mine was spewing gold, that might be. Now hush up about an airplane," she admonished him.

The time between the two holidays flew by. Jill was becoming more and more excited about having a baby. David, as well had started planning on a baby's room. They were trying not to get too excited until her first ultrasound, scheduled for early January. Her OBGYN had confirmed her pregnancy. She had already told Jill a bit about what to expect and about nutrition and cautioning her about alcohol consumption.

Soon they were back in Atlanta for Christmas. It was a grand celebration. David and Jill went to midnight services at her old church. David's parents joined them even though they were Methodists. It was very moving for all. David and Jill announced they had joined a church in Denver. They said that they had settled on Methodist since it was near where they lived and it had a lot of young people about their age. Both sets of parents were very approving.

As they had planned, they announced their good news to both families on Christmas day.

Excitement reined. The first to be told was Jill's parents.

"So, you two have given up on your Old Mill for a home, is that right?" Jill's dad asked.

"No, not at all dad. We love the Old Mill. We just don't want to be isolated there all winter, every winter. We also love Denver. I guess now is a good time to announce to you, mom and dad, David and I are expecting a baby this coming summer!" Jill said.

"Great! How wonderful," her mother said. "When are you due? So, moving to Denver does really make sense, though coming back here may have made more sense," Mary commented.

Jill responded, "Our baby is due in June."

"Oh, an anniversary baby. How wonderful," her mother commented

"David, have you told your folks yet?" Jason asked.

"Not yet, we plan to tell them tomorrow."

David's parents responded to their news in a similar way as Jill's, suggesting they should be near family when their baby arrived. David and Jill politely said they would think about that, though making no promises.

As expected, their families pressured them to return to the South. The pair politely declined, once again explaining they were Coloradoans now.

Back in Denver, they found the remainder of the winter, while cold at times and with some snow, was much more acceptable than holding up at the Old Mill. As David said, an additional five thousand feet of elevation makes a lot of difference, especially in winter.

That winter they focused on their new arrival coming in the summer, getting the baby's room finished and furnished. Jill was busy devouring books on child care when she wasn't preparing school lesson plans and grading papers. David even got into going with Jill to pick out maternity clothes. Jill was determined to stay healthy during her maternity. She and David spent a great amount of time walking in parks with Millie.

The big day arrived in early March. They were going for Jill's second sonogram. It was the one where they could find the sex of their baby. This event also brought the seascape painting back to their minds since in the painting the little boy appeared to be the older of the two children. Of course, Henry Mack couldn't have known the order of their children. They agreed it was only a fifty / fifty chance, still it would be interesting if their first turned out to be a boy. They didn't really have a preference.

"Say, how about twins?" David said as they walked into her doctor's office.

"Hush up, I can't be having twins."

As most expectant parents do, they had already picked out names for both a boy and a girl.

"Let's see if we are going to have a Jack or Julie," Jill said as her doctor prepared the ultrasound.

"Congratulations, looks like you are in for a little boy," the doctor announced as the pair pored over the copy of the image she printed out. David leaned over and kissed Jill as she still lay on the exam table.

21. The Seascape Painting

As the pair were driving back to their home from Jill's second sonogram, David commented on the possible match to the little boy in the Seascape painting.

"Well, that doesn't prove too much," Jill said, then added, "now if our second one just happens to be a girl, that may get more interesting."

The pending event did get David to refocus on solving the Seascape mystery.

"Back to the Seascape, how on earth are we going to find the location of that painting?" Jill asked.

"The way I see it we should look at the clues Henry gave us in the note, the message on the back of the painting, and those numbers. Those numbers must mean something. We just have to figure out what. Another thing, somehow, I feel either Bill Brooks or the Flanders probably have information we need to solve the mystery," David concluded.

"What do you think? When and where do we start?"

"How about right now, you know, we probably have only five years until our son will be the age of the boy in the picture, don't you figure?"

David said, "This is what I think we should do. Let's go

and see Bill Brooks. I am sure he knows more than he has told us. What do you think?"

"I agree. He should be where we start," Jill confirmed. "I am so excited for another quest."

It was 4 o'clock on Friday, January 14th, when the two once again walked into Bill's office for their appointment. They had only told Bill that they had a matter they felt he could help them with.

"Welcome, my favorite young couple," Bill said. "It's great to see you again. Jill, you look radiant. Does that radiant glow you have possibly mean you two are expecting?"

"We sure are and are thrilled about it," Jill responded.

"That is just wonderful. I am so glad for both of you. I am also glad that you two are now at least part time Denverrites. What can I help you two with today?"

"We are here about the Henry Mack 'Seascape' you gave us," Jill said.

David then spoke up, saying, "Jill and I have really enjoyed the painting. We discovered a note left by Henry in an old toolbox we found in the mine. From that note, and the message on the back of the painting, we believe there is another mystery that Henry has left for us to solve. We believe you may know more about the painting than you have shared with us."

"I see. I told you I did not know where the painting was done. That is true. I didn't tell you any more since I didn't want you to waste more time chasing an impossibility. Now that you seem determined about this, I will share with you what little more I know about the thing.

"About a year before Henry died, he brought me the

Seascape. He said he painted it on a trip back east. He told me a story about buying the painting's site through a local realtor. He said the ocean front property on both sides of the property had been sold to wealthy individuals with covenants that his property was to have no access through their properties, in order for it remain pristine.

"He then had me add an 's' to his trust he left for you. I took that to mean he intended this property to be included in his trust, only he never disclosed where it was or a legal description. I fear it is a loss cause. If I knew any more, I would tell you," Bill promised.

David asked, "Was there nothing in Henry's personal effects or papers about where the beach scene might have been painted?"

"Your great uncle was not very organized when it came to papers. Whenever I handled a transaction for him, it took a great effort for him, and me, to gather the necessary documents. I went thru his papers after his death in an effort to see if there were records of more properties, or trusts, for that matter. Having found none, I boxed up everything and sent it to my legal storage warehouse. You are welcome to look through it if you wish."

"Well, I guess that leaves us back near square one, but we didn't give up on the Old Mill and we aren't going to give up on this," David said.

"I am so sorry I can't be of more help with the painting. I wish I knew more. You two must let me know when your new arrival happens. Best wishes and if there is anything my wife or I can help you with, please call on us," Bill said as they were leaving.

Back home, David told Jill, the answer must still lie in the assortment of numbers. He just had to figure out what they meant. Then, a couple of days later, while studying the toolbox note, he had an epiphany. It was a nine number sequence. The same as a phone number, perhaps that was what it was. First, he looked up the first three numbers. They were a prefix for a North Carolina area code. Then it hit him, maybe it was the Flanders phone number.

David knew that Jill had kept the Flanders phone number in her I-phone. He would check it out just as soon as she returned from school.

"Jill, didn't you keep the Flanders phone number in the contacts on your phone? I need to know their number."

She promptly provided the number. Sure enough, it matched.

"This must mean something," David said. "Henry must have meant for them to inquire a bit more from the Flanders."

The next day, Saturday, both David and Jill dialed the Flanders number. They got them right away. They greeted each other and Jill announced she was pregnant. The Flanders both offered their congratulations.

David then told them that Henry's friend and executor, Bill Brooks, had given the pair a Seascape painting as a housewarming gift. They believed it might be the same one that Henry told them he was painting. Like their Old Mill paintings, this one also had a cryptic note on the back. They were now on the search for the location where he had painted it.

Jill said that when she and David had visited the Flanders at their home, they had related that Henry sent them a note about painting just such a scene. Now they were very anxious to see if their note from Henry might offer a clue to the location where it had been painted.

After a moment, Sarah Flanders said, "Yes, I do seem to remember the note Henry sent us when he was painting at the shore. I don't recall that he said where it was, but yes, I believe we saved it because he even painted a miniature picture of the shore on the note."

Jill, quite excitedly asked if Sarah thought she could locate it, as it might help with their search. She responded she would look for it in a box she had of papers from that timeframe. She promised to call them in a day or so when she found it.

A couple of weeks later, Sarah finally called back. She apologized for the delay, saying they had been called out of town right after they last spoke. Sarah announced that she in fact had found the note they talked about. She went on to say that she and Fred were going to Hawaii in a couple of weeks and they would stop off in Denver and see them before flying on the following day.

David and Jill promptly invited them to stay the night with them and that they would pick them up at the airport. The Colorado pair were thrilled. They fully believed the Flanders note was the clue they needed.

When they picked the couple up, amongst their luggage was a large suitcase affair made special for transporting paintings. It seemed they had brought the pair another painting to decorate their houses with. The Flanders said that now that they had two homes, more paintings might be nice. This one was by another artist, who Jill recognized as a famous painter and she was at once aware that it was quite a valuable thing. Both thanked them for their generosity.

Then Sarah produced the special letter from Henry with a miniature watercolor attached. She could immediately see it was the same location of their Seascape. David and Jill proudly showed Fred and Sarah their Seascape painting that Bill Brooks had given them. They really admired it and said they hoped the note from Henry might help them. Sarah did say she would like Henry's note back as a keepsake. David and Jill graciously agreed to return it.

Upon studying the little watercolor, David noted that curiously instead of Henry having signed it, there were three letters in the lower right corner. They read GPS. Immediately it hit him.

David said, "that is what I thought. The numbers are GPS coordinates. We now must just figure the coordinates out!"

The other take away from the Flanders note was the postmark on the envelope. It gave them a big clue to the general area. It was postmarked Port St. Joe, Florida. Looking at a map they found it to be a small town on the panhandle of Florida.

David again excitedly spoke up saying, "With this general location, we can track down the site."

The other two were not convinced that it would be possible, but Jill had faith in David's belief he could. Soon after their guests departed, David again started poring over the numbers he had. While back in Leadville that next week, he mentioned to Sam about their hunt and his having to divine GPS coordinates from a mass of numbers. Quickly, Sam became immersed in the puzzle.

The numbers they had to work with included those in the note in the old toolbox and those painted on the walls in the mine. Sam suggested that they should look up the coordinates of Port St. Joe and of sites along the beach to see if any matched any of their numbers. That was the idea that led to solving the location. Within days, David and Sam had pinpointed a possible location on the beach near Port St. Joe.

"Let's go to Florida," Jill chimed in.

"Not so fast. You need to finish out your school year and I think we should check with your doctor to see if it is ok for you to travel."

"Oh, I will be fine. I am not due for two months. You do have a good point about school, but that is over in two weeks. Then we go!"

Two weeks later, with Jill's classes over and having received cautionary approval from her OBGYN they made reservations to head South. Rather than flying into Atlanta and making a long drive to the beach, they opted to fly directly to Tallahassee, rent a car, and make the hour drive to the beach from there.

"Say Jillie, you going to be able to find a swim suit to fit that baby bump of yours?" he asked.

"You find me a private beach and I may go without a suit," she shot back. "If not, they do make swim suits for pregnant women, you know," his pert lass responded.

"Not as pregnant as you," he shot back.

On the plane flight to Tallahassee, the pair discussed whether the trip made sense. After agreeing it probably didn't, they laughed and made a toast to old Henry with a plain OJ for Jill and a vodka OJ for David. By the time the flight crew announced preparations for landing in Florida, Jill was asleep on David's shoulder, and he was nodding off as well.

Since it was already after 4 o'clock when they arrived, David suggested they find a hotel in Tallahassee for the night then go to the beach in the morning. The anticipation of what they might find made for a difficult night's sleep for David. Due to her pregnant condition, Jill as well failed to sleep soundly.

After an early morning breakfast at their hotel, the couple headed south to the coast. According to his GPS, David told Jill the drive should be a little over an hour. With the GPS he expected to be guided directly to the property. It wasn't quite that simple, since he wasn't a crow, and therefore couldn't travel in a straight line.

An hour and a half later they turned on a small road, without a sign other than Dead End No Outlet.

"David, are you sure this is right? This looks more like a driveway than a street," she said.

"Yes, I know but this is the direction to the referenced point. It shows it to be only a short distance further."

It wasn't too long before they came to a securely fenced estate with a gated driveway entry. There was signage along the fence stating Private Property. No Entry. They wondered if that could be it, but the GPS indicated the place they sought was a bit further down the road.

They kept driving. The fence to their left had now extended for over a mile. Ahead David could see another gate and drive, but no grand entrance as the last had been.

They stopped with the GPS indicating their arrival at their destination. The steel gate was securely padlocked. A large, nicely painted sign read, THE PAINTER'S ESTATE. Private Property, No Entry. Below the lettering there was a phone number. The pair gazed through the gate, seeing a narrow drive through palmettos with a stand of palms and what might be dunes in the distance.

Afraid to trespass, they elected to call the phone number listed on the sign. David found the number was that of a law office. He told the receptionist that he was inquiring about the Painter's Place and believed the owner was a relative of his. The receptionist then transferred him to one of their attorneys.

The man who picked up the phone, a Mr. Roth, assuming David was a developer looking to buy the plot, launched into a pre-learned speech that the property was not for sale as it was owned by a preservation trust. David was finally able to speak. He said, "No you don't understand, I think I may actually own this place." This possibility appeared to shock Mr. Roth, apparently that situation was new to him.

David went on to explain his story. The attorney still seemed a bit suspicious of the story but ended with, "If you are truly who you say you are, then yes, one of the firm's partners would likely want to speak with you."

Mr. Roth encouraged David to come to their office in

Tallahassee that afternoon. David said he would be there by 3 o'clock.

"So, Jill looks like a drive back to the big city."

"If that is what it takes," she said.

Upon arrival at the large law office, they asked for Mr. Roth, saying they had a 3 o'clock appointment. The meeting went well. Mr. Roth asked David for identification. They took note that the name Mack held a significance to him. Soon he left David and Jill alone for a few minutes. Upon his return he asked them to follow him to another larger office.

They then met with a Mr. Gary Hallman, a partner in the firm. He asked David to again relate his story. David showed him a picture of Henry's Seascape. Mr. Hallman then explained about the Painter's Trust that had been set up by his great uncle. As was the case in Colorado, it was an unusual affair. The expansive site involved a total of three properties, two developed ones and the center undeveloped parcel. The trust had been set up with a forty-year life, of which thirteen years remained.

The two developed properties were on land leased from the trust for the duration of the trust and they paid an annual rent of approximately fifteen thousand dollars a year each. Those funds were used to maintain the center vacant parcel and for security. According to the trust, at the end of the forty-year term, the entire property was to pass to the nearest living relative of Mr. Henry Mack. In this case currently David's father, though ultimately David.

David asked if he and Jill could get a key so they could go and look at the property. Mr. Hallman instructed Mr.

Roth to give him a key, saying he was welcome to keep it and use it whenever he wished. Mr. Hallman promised to stay in touch with David.

"Well, Jill, how about we spend the night here in Tallahassee then tomorrow finally see our Seascape," David suggested.

"Seems like a plan, my man!"

The next morning, gate unlocked, they slowly drove down the white limestone gravel and shell road. The road ended at the palms. They parked there, with ocean in sight they walked up onto the dunes and what they saw was a great expanse of untouched white sandy beach. The scene matched the painting perfectly, that is, minus the two children and their sand castle.

David said, "It is perfect, other than the children, of course."

Jill piped up. "We are sure working on that daddy! What say we take off our shoes and walk in the surf?"

"That's just what I was thinking, great suggestion."

"Wow, this feels wonderful. I could get used to this."

"Me too. We shall now add Seascape to our regular travel agenda," David said.

"Say, Jill, that day when we first met in Professor Murphy's office could you have imagined our journey these past four years?"

"I sure couldn't. You know if the next four years are as exciting as the last, I may not survive."

"Sure, you will! My love we are just getting started!"

They both agreed, all that they have is nothing compared to the value of their love. That was their real prize!

"I believe Henry and Carolyn would be happy for us as well don't you agree, Jill?"

"Sure do, I hope we can do for our kids and others what those two have done for us."

As the pair finished their surf walking and stood there again gazing at the scene, David and Jill had a long embrace. David then said, "You know, I have an idea that I might just get a metal detector and check out this beach. Do you thing there might be something under where Henry painted that Sand Castle?"

"Great idea, my dreaming husband, but let's wait until Jack and Julie are with us and they are the age of the kids in the painting. That is the way Henry would have wanted it, don't you think?"

"Beautiful Beach We Shall Return!"

Acknowledgements

Thanks to the talented artist, Susan Proctor for quickly doing the Seascape Painting on the back cover.

A special thanks to Rosemarie Perry for her tireless effort in reading and helping edit this book and my previous writing endeavors.

About the Author

The Old Mill Paintings is Larry Engels' third novel. Prior to his retirement Engels career was in construction management. During his career he built projects of all types over most of the U.S. Following a miraculous recovery from brain surgery he considered a new passion, writing.

Fifteen years ago, while on a trip to the Canadian Rockies he started his first novel. It was set in the history of the early days of the area. The author gained his knowledge from museums, other writers and even from the few old survivors of times past. That story was titled Trails Through Time. Though science fiction, that story incorporated a lot of the real events and people of the early twentieth century.

Over the subsequent two years since the publication of his first novel he decided to write a sequel titled The Music Box Treasure. It continues the story of Craig, now in the early twenty-first century. This story is written through the eyes of a couple of twenty-year-olds. While still an adventure, like his first book, this has the romance of two young people on an embarking on an exciting life together.

With this work *The Old Mill Paintings* the author was inspired by an oil painting of an Old Mill. He creates a romantic adventure of two college kids and their quest to locate the Old Mill in the painting. What follows, turns into a two-year search reaching from the hills of North Carolina to the Colorado Rockies and ending on a Florida beach.